DATE DUE

DEMCO 38-296

WHO DID WHAT TO FEDALIA?

BOOKS BY MEREDITH WILLSON

Who Did What To Fedalia?

And There I Stood With My Piccolo

Who

DID *What*

TO *Fedalia?*

BY MEREDITH WILLSON

Doubleday & Company, Inc., Garden City, N.Y., 1952

The characters and the incidents in this book
are entirely the product of the author's imagination
and have no relation to any person, or event in real life.

LIBRARY OF CONGRESS CATALOG CARD NUMBER 52-5228

This book is dedicated to Rini, Dixie, Cedric, and George

WHO DID WHAT TO FEDALIA?

CHAPTER ONE

Fedalia was house cleaning early one Saturday morning when the man brought the autoharp to the door. The boys were both peddling bills for the dry-goods store and Papa was down at the paper. She answered the bell with a wiping towel pinned around her small blond head. The salesman very solemnly said, "Ah, good morning, madam—are you the lady of the house?"

"Yes, sir," Fedalia said, realizing, somehow, for the very first time since Mama had passed away, that this was true.

"Then-may-I-invite-your-attention-to-this-miracle-of-the-music-world-recently-designed-and-patented-at-the-home-office-capable-of-transporting-the-members-of-your-household-to-an-hitherto-unexplored-world-of-beauty-on-wings-of-melody-with-no-necessity-for-an-expensive-academic-musical-educa-tion-called-The-Zimmerman-Wings-of-Magical-Melody-Auto-harp?"

"Yes, sir," Fedalia said again. "Won't you come in?"

"Ah—thank you," said the man as he stepped through the storm door. Carefully stomping his overshoed feet on the threshold, he continued on into the small front hall as far as the hall seat, where he sat down and removed his heavy cap with fur-lined ear flaps attached, as well as his leather mittens. He then proceeded, not without a certain ceremony, to undo the large cardboard box under his arm and disclose *The Wings of Magical Melody Autoharp*, which he placed upon his lap with a flourish. Then, with a disarming smile, almost as though he were yielding a great professional secret to a stranger in whom he had suddenly and impetuously decided to confide, he unwound his woolen scarf, opened his overcoat, reached through his sweater into a distant vest pocket, and produced a mandolin pick.

Without regard to time or rhythm he proceeded to pluck out what may have been intended for "In the Sweet By and By." At the end of his rendition, and with the strings still vibrating their jangle in the air, the gentleman smiled modestly and remarked that an overnight trial would be quite in order, after which a small down payment of three dollars and a half would perpetuate the magic of melody in that particular home, provided, of course, that an additional three dollars was available monthly for the next year.

"I will be in Fort Madison again tomorrow—no, tomorrow's Sunday. I'll stop by on Monday for your decision, madam—ah, miss—if that will be all right. May I wish you good day?"

"Yes, sir," Fedalia said for the third time, and as the overshoes went crunching down the walk she was saying to herself, with a speculative glance at the autoharp on the hall seat, "If I can't play a better tune on this machine than that gentleman just did, I will be very surprised."

Fedalia did not allow herself to touch the fascinating

musical instrument right away as she wanted to do. As Papa constantly reminded her and the boys, the only time you can successfully do two things at once is when you sleep and dream. "A division of interest is always weakening," was the way he put it.

So the ashes were shoveled from the parlor stove, the spillings carefully swept up from around its small door and metal feet; the tray underneath was emptied and the isinglass wiped clean, the coal scuttle filled from the shed side of the outhouse. The wooden seat in the adjoining side was scrubbed with the warm naphtha suds left over from the kitchen linoleum. The boys' stockings and underwear were taken in from the line—frozen stiff since early morning—and soon sizzled to normal shape on the ironing board, then folded away warm and dry in the third drawer of the commode in the side bedroom. The beds were made and the slop jars emptied—mittens, overshoes, stocking cap, and coat donned and doffed for each trip outside—just as the twelve o'clock whistle blew from the roundhouse. Fedalia hoped Papa's liverwoosht sandwich was thick enough this time and that the boys would be able to stop in somebody's kitchen to eat their dinner out of the weather.

She warmed up some of the breakfast oatmeal for herself and brought up some sauce from the cellar to have for dessert, along with two graham crackers. She wondered if anybody actually liked graham crackers.

Her early-afternoon routine included washing up the dishes before starting with the carpet sweeper and the dusting.

Today's cleaning had to last for two weeks because next Saturday she'd be working at the greenhouse all day, in addition to every afternoon after school, now that the first Christmas wreaths had to be made.

She finished with the bedrooms first, wondering—in view of the fact that she had long passed her thirteenth birthday—

if she couldn't change the pillow slips like Mama always did by holding the pillows under her chin, but still being too small, she ended up as usual doing them flat on the bed.

The dust rag on the end of the broom came out from under the beds dirty enough, as always, to require a separate shaking from the entry steps for each bed. She was tempted, as always, to leave her outdoor things on for the return trips back into the house but didn't. It was easier to catch cold inside with your things on than outside with them off, and it was so hard on Papa and the boys to do for themselves whenever she took sick.

When the dusting and the sweeping were finally finished it was already time for the supper potatoes to be peeled, the table to be set, and the margarine colored. Tonight was beefsteak, but she could pound it later and cut the bread while Papa was reading the paper.

Now then. She took off the wiping towel, carried the big teakettle with both hands into the side bedroom, poured enough hot water into the bowl to break the chill of the pitcher water, washed her hands and face, and went into the front hall. Picking up the autoharp from the hall seat, she carried it carefully into the parlor and sat on the edge of the sofa, putting the instrument down beside her. She first smoothed her dress like Mama always did before doing anything and then, after a moment of heart pounding, started poking gingerly at the little keylike hammers.

CHAPTER TWO

When Papa Parker opened the front door and heard his eldest child chirping "Sweet Genevieve" to her own accompaniment on the autoharp he dropped limply onto the parlor sofa in complete mistrust of his own ears.

Through supper and on into the evening the excitement grew with each new rendition, of which there were a considerable number. Papa called out into the cold night air at anybody who happened to pass by the house, neighbor or not, and insisted on their witnessing the phenomenal talent that had lain unnoticed in his own child's patient little bosom all these years. Folding boxes at the greenhouse indeed! Why, you should have seen her tuning those pairs of strings just right with the kitchen pliers. Who told her how to do that? Here was a genius—pure and simple.

"Oh, Papa, I don't know how I know the different strings need to be tuned up. I just hear them someway. Doesn't everybody?"

"Indeed they do not. You are just a natural-born musician, Fedalia, and you're goin' to get your chance with music lessons even if we all got to starve around here to see to it, ain't she, boys?"

"Yes siree, Papa," Ernie said. His older brother said, "You're darn right!"

"Now, Papa! We could never afford it——"

"We're goin' to afford it, sweetheart, and you better tell Mr. Quimby right away Monday after school that you ain't goin' to be able to help out at no greenhouse no more. You got to practice your singin'! You know what I'll do? I'll just have a little talk with Mr. Vance down at the music store to see about gettin' a piano!"

"Papa! A *piano!*"

"Maybe secondhand, but I'll manage it."

Fedalia shook her head. "But the greenhouse money, Papa . . . I better stay on there, at least this winter, hadn't I? Couldn't I practice my voice just the same?"

"Fedalia, a division of interest is always weakenin'. Don't you wanna be a great vocal singer for the Lord's sake?"

"Well, yes, Papa."

"Ernest, stop pokin' at that autoharp!"

"Aw, Papa. Maybe I got talent too. Mama had a keen ear, you always said. You always said she could——"

"*Ernest.* Never refer to your mother as 'she.' "

"Excuse me, Papa. You always said Mama——"

Papa pointed his finger at his daughter. "Fedalia, just you leave the flower business to them people who can't carry a tune, like Mr. Quimby. I ain't no genius, but I sure recognize one when I see one, and from now on we skimp and scrape till we get the cush for our little Fee to take music lessons!" Papa was getting so excited his voice cracked. He kept right on, speaking in the middle of a swallow. "Jess, how'd you like a *Post* route, just a few customers at first? You could handle it Thursday mornin's before school all right now, couldn't you, Son? And later on a few *Ladies' Home Journals* and *Country Gentlemen*?"

"Sure, Papa. I could——"

"And, Ernie, come summer, you can take over Fedalia's lettuce garden, only from now on the lettuce jar is the music-lesson jar!"

"Yes siree, Papa. Play another piece again, Fee, why don'tcha?"

Fedalia began playing and humming again and Papa kept right on talking through the music. "Wait till I tell 'em down to the paper—so high 'n' mighty, takin' for granted Red Parker couldn't never amount to nothin'. My own child a musical-singin' genius. My own flesh and blood! We'll make Fort Madison set up and take notice, I'll see to that!"

CHAPTER THREE

After school on Monday, Fedalia went out to the greenhouse for the last time to say good-by to Mr. Quimby and to Mrs. Burt and Henry and the green boxes and the glass and the fern. On the way home the big ice-covered oak trees moaned and creaked and Fedalia was soon running desperately as usual, making dabs at her nose with her mittens.

Papa said you have to sacrifice to be a big successful singer, Fedalia thought, panting with her last energy into the final block before being gathered in by the safe wooden arms of her own front porch. Probably that's why the Lord arranged for me to feel so bad about giving up the greenhouse.

She unbuckled her overshoes and took them out to the back entry to dry. Jody Sutlough was cutting through the back yard from next door.

"Come in, Jody," Fedalia said. "You shouldn't come through those drifts in the back yard."

"I'm goin' on seven and I will if I want to. Your father rang up on our telephone. He said you should take the autoharp down to the paper at six o'clock."

"Thank you, Jody. Did you know you had soot on your face?" Fedalia took out her handkerchief and moistened the corner of it with her mouth as Jody backed off.

"Don't want to be washed in spit."

"All right, then. Did your mother say you could have a cookie?"

"Yah, but I don't want no gingersnaps, see-stoo?"

"We only have gingersnaps, Jody."

"Ya got parafeen?"

"Only there on the ironing board."

"I'll have some, then."

Fedalia squeezed off a wad. "You're sure——"

"You got 'ny sugar for my parafeen?"

Fedalia held out the sugar bowl. Jody crammed the paraffin in his mouth first, followed it with a spoonful of sugar, and then went out the back door.

The autoharp slipped easily into its cardboard box, and Fedalia bundled up again, took the instrument in her arms, and started out as fast as she could. Snow sparkled under the street light at Brownell's corner and squeaked under her shoes. It was only five blocks to the paper, but her fingers were numb and her arms ached by the time she arrived.

She went out through all the noise into the back where Papa worked with the big boiling vat full of hot lead. The last time she came down she heard somebody say, "Red'll stick his finger in there for a dime." She wished they'd call him Mr. Parker instead of Red. Everybody knew Papa, though, and Papa knew everybody, even if he did have a hard time remembering their names. "Fedalia," he often told

17

her, "I'll positively guarantee that anybody who can call everyone they meet b' name has got to be a success. If I could do that I'd *be* somebody in this town."

She heard his voice now, loud over the machine noises. "She'll do what I tell her—always has. We Parkers are workers—hard workers. Sunup till sundown and the night chores after that. She'll practice her music just like her mother and her grandmother did their chores before her—sunup till sundown. They got it offen their folks and she gets it offen me. The name Parker's gonna mean somethin', I'll see to that. Yes, sir. By the time I get that typesettin' job they been promisin' me all these years I'll be settin' up plenty a' Fedalia Parker's New York doin's all over the front page. Yes, sir."

Papa was talking to one of the printing-press men, following him back and forth from the press to a rapidly growing pile of handbills standing by the alley door.

Fedalia couldn't tell whether the man was listening or not. Papa looked tired and thin and not very important in his black-stained overalls and skullcap with the feed-store advertising nearly all sweated away. She'd always been thin too. According to Papa, it was a Parker trait. Mr. Quimby said, "You thin ones make the best pallbearers."

As she waited by the basement steps Mr. Huntley, the manager of the Bijou, came in the back door and started carrying out armfuls of handbills to his truck steaming in the alley. Handbills for his picture show, that's what they were. Fedalia was pretty sure the girl who sold the tickets at the show was stuck on Mr. Huntley, because in front of him she always seemed to be acting superior and indifferent, when it was plain she wanted to act interested.

That's why Fedalia understood about Charlie Landry pushing her at Sunday school. He only did it so she'd notice him.

People always seemed to confuse being noticed with being liked. She wondered why it was so important to Papa to follow the printing-press man back and forth, shouting at him.

Mr. Huntley was beautiful. He was a cigarette feend, though. She could remember Mama saying that when she was little. Mama had always been nice to Mr. Huntley anyway, referring to the feend part of him more sorrowfully than critically.

Shining Mr. Huntley. Managing the Bijou Theater and being a cigarette feend, marching down the aisle with his short, quick, important steps to whisper instructions to the piano player. When he hurried across down in front, from one aisle to the other, he always bent over in a very important way so as not to let his head interfere with the rays that carried the picture to the screen. The rays always seemed to be full of sparkling dust and now and then a moth.

Mr. Huntley was an officer in the militia. She loved to watch him on Memorial Day, the way he'd get his troop all clanked around the corner of the courthouse into the street and then hold his sword tight against his side and run past his men up to the front again.

He used to march backward wonderfully, too, as they were nearing a corner, so the men could hear him call out the proper command. She wished she was old enough to remember his coming back from the war. She was pretty sure she would have been in love with him if it hadn't been for Charlie Landry.

Charlie Landry, small or not, would look just beautiful in a militia suit. Funny that Charlie never guessed about her sending him the valentine last year. It was fun, his not knowing, though—maybe by the time she got into high school she'd be able to send him a boughten one. . . .

"Hey, Fee!"

Papa was still shouting even though the newspaper machinery had stopped.

"Lemme Sapolio up a little over at the back sink and I'll be right ready."

"All right, Papa. . . ."

She saw Papa slip a couple of slabs of lead type in his pocket for the boys to melt at home. She followed him all the way back to the sink.

"Where are we going, Papa, and did Jody get it right about the autoharp?"

"Yes-siree-sir, just exactly right, sister. We're going over to Farmer Garvey's." Papa was still yelling from habit until he mentioned Farmer Garvey. Then he dropped his voice. Everybody in town did. Papa rolled up his inky sleeves.

Going to see Farmer Garvey. That probably meant to borrow some money to pay down on the piano. And Papa probably thought Fedalia should play and sing something for Mr. Garvey to show him what a good thing it would be to loan them the money.

Papa washed in a hurry and covered up his overalls with his heavy coat, and in a few minutes they were shouldering their way into the wind, catty-corner under the street light at the Baptist Church corner. It was blowing up again. Fedalia couldn't tell if it was still snowing or not because either way the wind frosted you over good. The snow swirled around under the street light, pretty and flashing the way it drifted up on the library steps. Her nose froze and unfroze with every breath.

She got behind Papa after a while and followed his tracks, closing her eyes about a third of the time.

CHAPTER FOUR

Mr. Garvey's walk had been shoveled already and was starting to get drifted over again. Papa stomped on the walk. Fedalia did too. Then they went up on the porch and stomped again. They went into the storm entry and ground the bell handle. Mr. Garvey came to the door with his napkin in his neck. "Who is that out there?"

"Red Parker, Mr. Garvey. Got Fedalia with me. Didn't mean to get here so late as to interrupt your supper, but——"

"Now, Red, that's just all right. You and your young one come right on into the dinin' room. Emma's in the kitchen. I've saw about all I care to of the *Gazette* and I was just finishing up a extry bite a' supper. I'll swear, Emma got a good scald on that yellow cake tonight. Have a piece?"

Fedalia followed Papa and Mr. Garvey into the dining room off the front hall.

"We don't want to keep you, Mr. Garvey, but you see——"

"The last time I saw you, Fedalia, you was five pounds lighter'n a straw hat. You've growed like a milkweed, haven't you?" Mr. Garvey sat down at the table.

"Well, Mr. Garvey——"

"I'm just an old Iowa farmer, young one, but you mark what I tell you; catch yourself a good steady Iowa spriggins and settle down here in this state, never mind the extremes in the weather. Take out there tonight. Before mornin' it'll be snowin' till 'who laid the rails,' but it keeps folks hardy, fightin' off that stuff year in, year out. Like me and all my kin before me. Course, I know you're pretty young to be jawed at about settlin' down. What are you, Fedalia—thirteen —fourteen?"

"Yes, sir."

"Your head gets more gold onto it ever' time I lay eyes on you, young one. I like the way you always look right at a body, though I never could tell whether your eyes were blue or brown. Little a' both, mebby? Could that be? I'll swear the young ones grow clear out a' sight, seems like, right while you're lookin' at 'em. But you can't make plans too soon. Can you, Red?"

"No, sir, Mr. Garvey. That's the main reason——"

"Take that young Haversmith boy from up in Butler County. His people didn't have nothin' after they'd heired that farm from old man Haversmith. Let the thing run clear down to rack and ruin. You knew 'em, didn't you, Red?"

"No, I don't——"

"The kind a' people that was too poor to get a cow and too proud to keep a goat. They heired the farm and then spent ten years tryin' to run it fancy instead of good honest black-dirt furrow farmin'. Oh, they was nice enough. Ever' time I's in their neighborhood I'd stop in for a meal come noon or sundown and they'd set down as purty a bait a' victuals on their table as you'd ever see. But one mortgage was ridin' on the back of another till hell won't have it again. . . . You know how that is, Red—borrowin' with no hope of payin'."

"I know, Mr. Garvey. Now Fedalia brought along——"

"But this young Haversmith spriggins grew up while all this was going on, and one fine day he gradually started to get a little law and order around the farm, made his folks quit spendin' money they didn't have, tried to save a mite here, a mite there, figured out to get two crops, mebby, where they'd been lucky to get one before, and first thing you know, he went to a barn-dance affair and met that purty little Doerflinger girl. You know her people, Red?"

"Well——"

"They come from Hardin County, I believe, or could it-a been the Doerflingers from way up in Cerro Gordo? Anyway, he took her back over there to Butler County with him, married and all, and today the mortgages are cleaned up and they got all modern buildin's and even a Number Eight Cadillick with a self-beginner!"

"Now ain't that fine? That's how it goes, Mr. Garvey, when——"

"Was that Emma callin'? I promised I'd show her where to move her washin' machine out a' the furnace room. Set down yonder in the sittin' room, Red—you and the young one, if you care to. I've saw the *Gazette*. Help yourself. Though I guess you seen enough of it over at the printin' office, hey, Red?"

Fedalia said, "You aren't going to lend Papa any money, are you, Mr. Garvey?"

Papa got up suddenly and he and Mr. Garvey started talking at the same time. Mrs. Garvey called from back in the kitchen.

Farmer Garvey yelled back, "Jest a minute, Emma! What you sayin', Red?"

"It was just for a down payment on a piano, Mr. Garvey. You see, Fedalia has got quite a music talent for singing. She's got to learn music and we thought—I thought——"

Mr. Garvey cleared his throat loudly. "Well—now this is somethin' to talk over—I dunno . . ."

Papa spoke quickly. "Fifteen dollars would do it, I think, Mr. Garvey."

"Fifteen dollars, Red?"

"Well, now I think so, Mr. Garvey. Fedalia brought along her autoharp."

"Wrap yourself up, young lady. I'll swear, you're going to be a handsome woman one a' these days. Don't know as I take to that music for a business, though. But whatever you do, work hard at it and you'll wind up as safe as a toad in God's pocket. Yes, Emma, I hear you. I s'pose I could let you have fifteen, I guess, Red. See me downtown tomorrow."

Fedalia left Papa at Mr. Vance's house and went on home to start supper. A piano! Right there in their own house! She hadn't been surprised that Mr. Garvey did all the talking. She had noticed that the man with the advantage always did most of the talking. Papa, for his part, did *all* the talking the time Mr. Monroe stopped by to pick up the old overcoat Papa said he could have.

She ran most of the way and burst into the house, automatically calling to the boys to wash their hands. Everything was ready and on the table when Papa came pounding into the house.

"Sister! Mr. Vance has got a fine piano in mind for us, and in a few weeks I'll make the down payment and they'll move the piano right in that very day!"

"Papa! Honest?"

"Not only that, but Mr. Purdy was over takin' supper at Vance's, and he said Jess was old enough to help out foldin'" the news section into the paper Sunday mornings and maybe he could also do a little deliverin' around on his sled just before Sunday school."

"Gee, Papa, honest?" Jess said.

"That's right, my boy."

"Why can't *I*, Papa? Why can't *I*?"

Papa said, "Ernie, be quiet and eat your supper. Fee, there's somebody on the porch."

Fedalia went to the door, straightening her apron. It was the autoharp man. Fedalia said, "Good evening, won't you come in?"

The salesman was apparently more accustomed to taking back the instrument than selling it, because he didn't unwind his scarf or loosen his overcoat as he stepped into the hall. Papa came out and had hardly begun to explain about getting a piano in a few weeks before the gentleman was putting the cardboard box under his arm.

Considering the approaching holidays and also how the gentleman had been so important in the discovery of her talent, Fedalia was glad when Papa said, "Wouldn't you care for a dish of sauce before you go on?"

"And a cookie?" Fedalia added eagerly.

The gentleman said, "No, thank you very much. It isn't at all necessary. Good evening."

CHAPTER FIVE

Charlie didn't want to be taller just to be taller. He knew why he wanted to be taller. He wanted to be taller so he could do something ath-a-letic for the school and get to be a letter man, that was all. Well, that wasn't all; it was all only as far as his size was concerned. He still wanted his own mackinaw and he still wanted to kiss Fedalia Parker.

"Charles!"

"Yes, Mother."

"Take some hot water out of the teakettle and go upstairs and wash your neck and ears if you're going to go to Hyperian with me tonight."

"Yes, Mother." He wished his mother would call him "Charlie." Still, it was better than "Runt," like they called him at school. "Stub" wouldn't have been so bad. Not as bad as "Runt." "Midge" would have been all right, too, like "Midge" Birney.

"Did you hear me, Mr. Charles Landry? Come out from behind that door. I'm not going to address you again. That's word with the bark on it!"

"Yes, Mother." Here he was, a freshman in high school, and his measuring marks hadn't changed in over a year.

Charlie came out from behind the door. He preferred to do his measuring by himself—when nobody else was in the room. Aw, what's the use measuring, anyhow? He was a *runt*, that's all, and it looked like he was going to stay that way.

He hurried up the back stairs with the hot water, scooping up a fingernailful of frost off the window in the back hall where there wasn't any register. Winter wasn't any fun any more, though—not since he had to wear his sister's mackinaw. Everybody could instantly tell the difference between a boy's mackinaw and a girl's mackinaw. Red and black, first of all, was usually a girl's color, wasn't it? Maybe not, but anyway the small collar that hooked around the neck was a giveaway, a dead giveaway. The mere fact that his mother had taken off the small square flaps from the pockets and said, "It's just the thing!" hadn't impressed him at all. Couldn't they see how that high girl's collar had made his neck rough and chapped under his chin? Besides, when a guy was short to begin with, he needed all the help he could get with *masculine* things to make him appear not quite so short. That first miserable day he'd had to wear the thing to high school he'd told the kids it was because of the school colors being red and black. Trying to get across the idea that he had a much better coat at home. But of course Shink Burns had to stick in with something about was he going out for the girls' volleyball team in his spare time.

"Charles! Do you want me to give your turn to Marbella?"

Charles had already tried his best to give his turn to his sister. Anyway, it would have hurt his mother's feelings. She was always saying, "I got these tickets from the Little-I-had-

27

left-me in my uncle Ed's inheritance. Just so you children could have some appreciation of music and literature, so you'll stand out if you ever go to college. Though I prob'ly won't be here by then." His mother always liked to end on a sort of sad note whenever possible, usually saying the last couple words on an inhale, which made it sound more hopeless. The program tonight was going to be "Africa, the Dark Continent." How was that going to make him stand out at college?

Marbella's turn had been a lecture about science, including gyroscopes. A gyroscope was like a big top, as big as the double boiler, Marbella said, and they got a man out of the audience to try to hold that big top in his arms after it was all wound up, but he couldn't hold it and it pulled him right down to the floor!

"Charles! Do you want me to come up there? You'd think that after the way I took the Little-I-had-left-me, just to buy the Hyperian tickets for you children, you'd think that you would have the kindness to be ready on time."

"I'm coming."

Charlie and Fedalia were only in one class together and that was Current Events, and ever since Valentine's Day he'd been trying every way he could think of to get a look at her handwriting. He'd only received one ten-center, with practically real lace that folded and collapsed as you opened her out, and there was a handwritten verse inside which said:

> You may be small but I feel myself yielding.
> You're the nicest boy in the whole School Building.
>   Guess Who

Charlie wanted that valentine to be from Fedalia more than anything he could ever remember wanting. It coulda been a joke, though. It coulda been a razz. Oh no—not for any ten cents. Anyway, he could tell if he saw her handwriting.

Miss Morrisey, the Current Events teacher, grabbed her handbag and hurried out right after class to faculty meeting. And there on her desk were the class's papers. All in a pile, folded down the middle with the names on the outside. Charlie had quite a time with an imaginary piece of gum on his shoe till the coast was clear; then he grabbed for the pile. Fedalia's paper was about the fifth down from the top and there wasn't any doubt about it! Boy, oh boy, he knew all the letters on the valentine by heart, and the tender hand that wrote that poem also wrote this Current Events paper and signed Fedalia Parker to the bottom of it! Great Honk!

Shink Burns was standing by Fedalia's locker outside the assembly room as Charlie ran out into the hall. Fedalia looked at him with a wonderful smile, straight at him with those brownish-blue eyes, the way she did. "Hello, Charlie," she said.

"You mean Runt," Shink said. "Just plain Runt Landry. Can't you tell by looking at him?"

"Aw, I am not, Shink. And you can shut up." Charlie walked on down the hall. What else could a guy do? Couldn't pick a fight in front of a girl like Fedalia Parker. What good would it do to make such a spectacle of yourself? He kicked his way home with a Carnation milk can, playing foot-shinny and feeling rotten. If they gave a letter for foot-shinny, he'd sure be a big hero.

Well, what else could he do? There was no school baseball team, even if he could have made it. Basketball was out, of course. His hands were too small and he couldn't jump or throw with those big guys. Football. How about Cousin Clell's moleskin football suit with the nose guard you held in your mouth? Cousin Clell would loan it to him any time he wanted, and it was a darb all right, a real darb. A little big everywhere, but football suits were supposed to look big on you. At least they did on everybody else.

His only chance would be quarterback, of course. Midge Birney was a quarterback and he was pretty small too. It seemed like it was advantageous to have a quarter small enough to hide right under the center's big rear end and even sneak between his legs when a yard or so was necessary for a first down. Well, Great Honk, he could walk right between big Jim Weston's legs practically standing upright.

The first day of spring practice he thought he'd just arrange to sort of show up in Cousin Clell's moleskins without formally mentioning anything to the coach about his going out for the team.

Shink started it off, of course. Showing off just because he was the regular left halfback.

"Hey, guys! Will you take a look at *Runt!*"

"How many times I gotta tell ya my name's Charlie?"

"*Gee-ly Kly*, Runt, I never give you credit for such a sense a' humor!"

"Aw, you never mind, anyway." Charlie started away.

"Judas H. Priest! Lookie them moleskins! And that nose guard!"

Everybody around laughed, of course, and Shink kept on screaming his brains out and hollering like that, so naturally nobody was going to take a guy seriously and the only thing to do was go home. When he recognized Fedalia and her music roll coming up the street on the way to her music lesson it was too late to back up or cut down the alley.

"Hello, Charlie," she said. "Goodness, won't you get hurt trying to play football?"

"Why would I? Great Honk. Girls are sure dumb."

"Well, I sure hope you don't get hurt. Did you like the valentine?"

"Aw, it was all right, I guess." He turned his back and

hulked away, trying to look as masculine as possible under Clell's big moleskin shoulders. He knew Fedalia wouldn't have expected him to act any other way. Boys were always expected to be good-and-mean to girls, except maybe when they were alone together someplace or walking home from church maybe, with nobody around.

"I sure hope you don't get hurt." She said it right like that, looking straight at him, and she admitted sending the valentine, right straight out!

Well, that settles it. Yessir. If he was going to have a girl like Fedalia Parker he had to hurry up and be somebody.

Debating!

He wasn't any whiz in public speaking, but maybe if he went at it good and hard . . . They were going to have a public-speaking competition in the assembly room the last day before spring vacation, and the winners would represent the school next fall and get a letter! That gave him about ten days to get ready. You could read anything you wanted, a poem or anything. He'd enroll first thing tomorrow and learn that *Highwayman* poem, really learn it good, backward and forward if necessary! If he could just figure out a way to do it different. . . .

He sneaked up to the attic the minute he got home to start practicing, and before he could get used to the dark he stumbled over his father's Spanish-American Springfield leaning up by the window. *Great Honk!* Why not make up some kind of costume and carry that rifle and maybe even *shoot it!* Right at the climax! What an idea! They must have some blanks over at Gilbert's store because the Gilbert kids shot one off last Fourth.

The day before the competition Charlie had everything figured out. All he had to do was watch his chance after school and take over Cousin Clell's moleskin football pads and Gramma's purple shawl, Father's National Guard hat, and the Springfield, and hide all that stuff in his locker.

Next morning he asked Mrs. Samser if he could stay out in the hall till he was announced. He hinted that he might wear a costume for dramatic effect, and Mrs. Samser said, "Fine!"

Practically everybody in the school was in the assembly room, and Charlie was about number ten on the program so he had the gym to himself and plenty of time to get dressed up. He was ready and back upstairs with time to spare. He could hear everything that went on in the assembly room through the hall door, and he could also see Fedalia through the glass—in the front row!

He hung Cousin Clell's shoulder pads around his shoulders, then draped Gramma's purple shawl all the way across, just like a bandit's cape. His father's hat stayed on fine with a roll of paper in under the band. Mr. Benz had given him a charcoal mustache down in the basement at the last moment.

As he heard his name being announced he pulled back the trigger on the Springfield, which gave him a comforting view of the brass cap on the end of the blank cartridge, and strode through the door and onto the platform.

He ignored the rolling sound of appreciation that spread over the hall and, bowing very quickly, he hurried right into the first stanza.

" 'The wind was a torrent of . . .' *The Highwayman* by Alfred Noyes . . . uh . . .

"The wind was a torrent of darkness among the
    gusty trees . . .
Uh . . . The moon was a galley gostion, uh . . . a
    ghostly galleon tossed upon cloudy seas . . .
Uh . . . The ribbon . . . uh . . . the ribbon . . . uh . . .

32

the road *was* a ribbon *of moonlight on the purple*
moor . . .
Uh . . . And *the highwayman came riding riding riding*
up to the old inn . . ."

There was no doubt about it—Charlie did not know this
poem. He had been so excited about the costume and the
stanza where the gun went off that he realized with a terrible
sinking feeling that he had not what you'd call really mem-
orized the verses at all. He'd just have to skip over to the
shooting. He hadn't better say "breast," though. His mother
always referred to a woman's chest where her heart was as
"bust."
" 'TLOT-TLOT, in the frosty silence!' " He raised his
voice with confidence.

> *"TLOT-TLOT, TLOT-TLOT in the echoing night!*
> *Nearer he came and nearer!*
> *TLOT-TLOT . . . uh . . .*
> *She was going to warn him with her death!*
> *TLOT-TLOT TLOT . . . uh . . . TLOT . . .*
> *Her finger moved and the musket ruined her bust!"*

The Springfield was in good condition. It went off with the
loudest indoor noise since Crappy Crawford shot off a string
of cannon crackers in the cold-air ventilator. There was quite
a lot of smoke, too, and he wouldn't have been able to con-
tinue even if he could have thought of any more lines to say.
Charlie kind of avoided Fedalia for the next day or two.
Track was absolutely the only thing left, and what could
he do on the track team? There was the high jump, the broad
jump, the dashes, the distances, and the hurdles. Hmmm. He
must have left out something. He did: the hammer, the
discus, and the pole vault. . . .
Of course there was always the cross-country. They gave

you a letter for that. In fact, you got a letter for the first three places, and they gave them to you at assembly right the next week after the race, that being the last event of the school year! The cross-country! *Great Honk!*

When spring began to turn into early summer Fedalia and her father sometimes went to church at night. Charlie didn't want to set any dangerous patterns around his house with respect to going to church twice on a Sunday, but he dropped in the idea just offhand during supper. His mother was so surprised and pleased that she smiled and nodded all through the sermon, which didn't fit the hell-fire Reverend Tower was talking about any too well.

On the way home the Parkers were only a half a block ahead of them when they got to the street light on the corner.

"I . . . uh . . . guess I'll go on, Mother . . . if you don't care . . . uh . . . just to say hello to Fedalia Parker, just for a couple minutes." Charlie caught up with Fedalia and then he didn't know exactly what to say, so he tipped his cap and hurried right on past.

"Well, Charlie Landry! Aren't you even going to say hello?"

"Oh sure . . . uh . . . Hello, Fedalia. Hello, Red—Mr. Parker."

"Good evening, Charlie." Mr. Parker turned around. "Evening, Mrs. Landry."

"How are you, Mr. Parker?" Charlie's mother said with her trill. "We missed you in church last Sunday."

Mr. Parker said, "Hope you said a good word for me."

Mrs. Landry said, "Now, Mr. Parker. You know a seraph can pray for a sinner, but a sinner's got to pray for himself." Everybody laughed.

Fedalia said, "Can Charlie and I walk ahead, down to the bridge and back, Papa? It's such a real nice evening."

"Well, only fifteen minutes, Fedalia," her father said.

There weren't any street lights between the Parkers' house and the bridge, and it seemed like this was maybe the time when you didn't have to treat a girl mean. You could begin to try to treat her like you really felt about her.

Neither of them said anything as they turned around at the bridge. A little way back up the street Charlie let his hand swing along next to hers, and in the darkest place before they got to her house he took *hold of it!* "I'm going to get a letter, Fedalia," he said very fast. "By next week. *You'll* see."

"Why, Charlie! You are?"

"A fellow always ought to do something for . . . well . . . you know . . . uh . . . to show his girl, like a letter. So she can be . . . oh, I don't know. Gilbert's store always gives you a big red turtle-neck sweater to wear your letter on."

"Charlie . . ." Fedalia was looking right at him like she did. "I can't be your girl . . . really, that is . . . until we kiss each other. But I like you enough to, Charlie."

"Your old man is on the porch there in the swing." Charlie's voice broke right in the middle of the word "swing." He forced himself to keep talking. "You wait, Fedalia. You just wait. You'll see."

Mr. Parker called from the porch.

"That you, Fedalia? Better come in now. Good night, Charlie."

"Good night, Mr. Parker. Well, then . . . good night, Fedalia."

He sure wanted to squeeze her hand once, but he didn't dare with Mr. Parker right there in the swing. He went on down the street, starting to run almost immediately. What a girl! What a wonderful girl! She might-a kissed him too! She would-a kissed him! She said so!

The rest of the week finally ended and the cross-country wasn't a far-off rosy dream, it was *tomorrow!* He thought suddenly about those hard hairy pistons Shink Burns used for legs. Hooked onto his knees like they were jointed on there by a plumber. Well, maybe not first place or second. But third, anyway . . . Big "Moose" Felt didn't even finish last year, a big guy like Moose. Moose came as far as the corner of the school alley within sight of the finish line and then just fell down and got sick. All over his track pants and his tennis shoes. *Great Honk!* Tennis shoes! What was he going to run in? He didn't have any tennis shoes. Track pants they'd give him. But you had to furnish your own shoes. How about Cousin Clell's football socks? They'd shrunk so from washing they fit him pretty good and there were two pair. He'd wear them both and no shoes at all. Make his feet feel light as wings!

Charlie tried to run his race in his mind that night before going to sleep. It was about six miles, they said. He'd never run more than a mile all at one time without a stop. But this was different. He'd start out more carefully and save his wind, and then—well, just keep going. Just keep going. No matter what anybody else did. Just keep going and he'd win. . . . Well, third place, anyway. He practiced getting up from one knee in his mind maybe a hundred times before going sound asleep out of sheer nervous exhaustion. . . .

It is certainly a nice day for it, Charlie thought as he walked into the locker room next day. Shink Burns had on a regular track shirt with a red diagonal stripe across it and he had real track shoes in his hand, with spikes. "Runt!" he hollered out with a big guffaw. "You got some sensa humor! Judas H. Priest, will ya lookie them track pants! Down to his knees!" Well, of course everybody laughed. What could you expect? Charlie knew he looked funny, but Shink didn't have to chase him all over the gym trying to step on his stocking feet. Mr. Samser drew the route on the blackboard and went over it quite a few times. Then they said, "Everybody out in back to the starting line!" It looked like about sixteen starters, and they pushed the crowd back so everybody could start at the same time. Charlie didn't look around much. He didn't want to see Fedalia till it was all over.

"On your mark!" Mr. Samser had his real pistol in his hand. Everybody got down on one knee and so did Charlie. Somebody hollered out, "Hey, Coach, whyn't ya use the runt for your football mascot instead of that stinkin' goat?"

"Get set!" Even Mr. Samser was laughing when he said it.

Bang! The track shoes and tennis shoes started to scrunch off down the alley out into the road. Everybody seemed to be loping instead of running—long loping strides—and Shink Burns's red stripe was way up in front. Charlie tried to save himself and lope, too, but it seemed like he had to just put his head down and wind up his short legs as fast as he could to keep up with the bunch. Just as well. He was perfectly happy to get out of sight of that crowd at the starting line in a hurry. So he was a comedy mascot, was he? They'd all think that for sure if he fell out along the way and didn't finish. All right, then, he wouldn't fall out along the way. He'd finish. He had to, didn't he?

He'd been so embarrassed about all that yelling at the start that he hadn't let down at all yet, and he was still winding up his legs and unwinding them as fast as he could. Well, what do you know, the Christian Church already! That was nearly a mile from the school building and he wasn't last, either. He was in front of at least six or seven guys. They were all loping, though. Maybe he could try to lope now. He lengthened his stride, or tried to, and found it didn't work at all. He didn't have anything to lengthen! Any more than that little sausage dog of Mr. Malthouse's next door. He felt a panic inside him, shortening up his breath. How much longer could a guy just wind and unwind like that, like the Katzenjammer kids in the funny paper, tearing along as tight as he could tear along, lickety-split all the time? How much longer could a guy do that? Well, till you got back to the high school alley again, that's how much longer. Five more miles. Nobody was going to get in his way and make him stop, like in a football scrimmage. You're sure a runt, you Runt Landry. You sure are. Well, then, come on, Runt. Keep moving. . . .

He could hear himself breathing, not just breath sound but a real noise in his throat. Moose Felt's big shoulders disappeared around the corner of the pesthouse barn up ahead. That's nearly halfway to the halfway mark! It *is* halfway! A good mile and a half, maybe a little more! Seems like Moose would be too big to run.

Moose always reminded him of Mr. Wheeler's great Dane that he'd taken care of all last summer. That dog was too big to run too. He remembered the day that dog nearly died trying to catch him over in the south part of town riding with Rog Gilbert in the dry-goods store's Hupmobile. Boy, he sure knew exactly how that dog felt.

He passed the pesthouse barn, and then the pesthouse. Then downhill toward the railroad trestle, but it was almost harder going downhill than going up. His knees got to trembling all over. There was Moose Felt just ahead. The embankment in front of the trestle was just over Moose's hunched-up shoulders. After the trestle came the waterworks. Halfway! Well, what about it? He couldn't keep on any longer, nobody could, feeling like this. Maybe this numbness he was feeling was that second wind he'd always heard track guys tell about. . . . His feet weren't numb, though. They felt hot. Very hot . . .

How much more? Oh, not very much. Only a long mile

to the ball park, a mile to the greenhouse, half a mile to the planing mill, and five more blocks to the finish. Great Honk . . .

His feet felt like they didn't have any socks on or anything, pounding down on the dry road. Cousin Clell's socks would never be the same. He guessed the bottom pair was worn clear through because the toe part kept flapping back. He hadn't been breathing air for quite a while; he'd been gasping in fire. He'd had stitches in his side before, but not like this. There were stitches all through his stomach now, and in his lungs, and through both sides.

Well, there was the ball park, anyway, and four guys were ahead of him, Moose, then two guys he didn't know who they were, and then Shink way up in front with his red stripe. Nobody would ever believe the comical mascot had gone as far as the ball park with the first four guys. Shows you what you can do, I guess. And now I think I'm entitled to quit. I sure am entitled . . . He could tell Fedalia he lasted till the ball park. Maybe she'd believe him and maybe she wouldn't. . . . It wasn't good enough for her, though. It sure wasn't good enough just to stick it out to the ball park for a heavenly person like Fedalia. And what about the letter and the big red sweater? Even if he had to wear Marbella's mackinaw next winter he could hold it open if he had a letter, with his hands in his pockets.

How was it he'd pulled up to Moose again? Moose sure looks like he'd like to quit. Right now. Charlie hoped he *would* quit. . . . He *hoped* and *hoped* he would. Then he could quit right alongside Moose. . . . Nobody could keep going like that any more now. You just *couldn't*, that's all.

Moose quit all of a sudden, without a word! Just quit and walked along gasping like a big mountain. Charlie tried to quit, too, in a way. Actually he begged himself to stay right there with Moose. They could walk back together. No disgrace to quit right in front of Moose Felt. . . . All right, he'd quit—right now. . . .

Funny how he kept right on going, though. He'd decided to quit, hadn't he? *The greenhouse!* Well, that's plenty far enough. Give up, Runt, give up. You're going to die, Runt. Your heart is going to swell up any minute now and explode, along with the pounding in your neck . . . banging in your head. Can't even see good . . . A person can't sprint for six miles. Nobody can. You're not a runner, you Runt you. What did you come out here for, anyway? Maybe walk for a ways now? Or lope like the others? Just from here to that grocery store. Just to get one breath, like when you're drowning. . . . You're sure entitled to one gulp of air. . . . You'd fall down if you stopped, though. Never get up. Fall down. Right there on that old square brick sidewalk . . . Fall down, Runt. Give up. *Got* to . . . *Got* to . . . Could that be the *planing mill?* There's sure a whole lot of people standing along the street. Looks like everybody in Fort Madison. All the way from the planing mill to the high school! Didn't he fall down back there? Sure he did—no, he guessed he didn't. Was he still winding and unwinding like Mr. Malthouse's little sausage dog, lickety-split? Like the Katzenjammer kids? Guessed he was. Clell's socks were sure finished, clear through to his feet. His feet were two ragged packages on top and fire on the bottom. He'd have to throw up now, sure. Awful double stitch inside there someplace. He sure was going to have to puke. *Right now.* Couldn't puke and keep on running, though. That would look ridiculous. Here it comes. I guess I'll strangle, vomicking up when I can't breathe even. . . . There's the red stripe just ahead. Where's such a racket coming from? Well, Shink, your hairy pistons are going up and down, aren't they? Up there in front of me. No they're not either going up and down. They're going horizontal—more like pistons are supposed to. Like at the waterworks. Why are you on your hands and knees, Shink? How could you fall down when I'm still winding and unwinding? I guess I'm going on by you, Shink. Before it's too late. Got to . . .

"Charles, aren't you getting taller? Or is it just the way you look with that turtle-neck on?"

"I don' know, Mother. I don't measure myself any more."

"You're not planning to wear that sweater to the church recital tonight, are you?"

"Yes, Mother."

"In this weather?"

"Yes, Mother."

"Well, get ready then. After spending the Little-I-had-left-me, just to get the tickets for you children, it does seem as though you could be on time."

"I thought the tickets were free tonight."

"There'll be no impudence from you, young man. Now as soon as you're ready I'll be waiting on the porch."

The screen slammed and Charlie heard his mother's voice in a different pitch. "Hel-lo there, Mrs. Purdy. We missed you in church last Sunday."

Mrs. Purdy called cheerfully from the walk, "Why, thank you, Mrs. Landry. I hope you said a wee prayer for me?"

"Now, Mrs. Purdy. You know a seraph can pray for a sinner, but a sinner has to pray for himself."

Both ladies laughed delightedly and exchanged temporary good-bys. Mrs. Purdy couldn't have been out of earshot when Charlie heard his mother's pleasant tinkle again. "Charles dear—it's getting la-ate."

CHAPTER SIX

The family hadn't paid any attention to Fedalia's birthday because of the recital coming in the same week. That was perfectly all right, because a division of interest right at that particular time would certainly be dangerous. How wonderful it was that such a fine piano teacher as Mrs. Wilmert lived right in Fort Madison.

Mrs. Wilmert had constantly reminded her to be prepared to perform at the recital without the music, so she'd been practicing "The Glow-Worm" from memory. She was late to her lesson last Saturday, waiting as long as she possibly could for Charlie to come out of the high school after the race. He wasn't at church either, and their Current Events class was canceled Monday for the assembly when they gave Charlie his letter.

She wanted so badly to see him alone to tell him how proud she was of his winning, but the whole week had gone by without that chance because Papa had kept her out of school the rest of the week to practice. Maybe Charlie would be at the recital tonight and she could see him after, while Papa would be accepting congratulations.

She hadn't done too well this morning at the dress rehearsal, but she'd be all right tonight. She wished the dresser mirror would tip down so she could see if the white dress hung evenly at the bottom. She hoped Charlie would come. She didn't think she'd be nervous like so many others she'd seen who went pale, just speaking a piece at school, but she had felt dry in her mouth all day and fluttery, even, and couldn't seem to remember. Her face felt hot and cold at the same time, and even in her stomach she felt strange.

She must know "The Glow-Worm" better than anybody in the world after practicing it so hard, and yet, in her mind, she couldn't place her hands on the keys right at all. She was going to give the "Fairies" piece as a vocal encore with Mrs. Wilmert at the piano, but when she practiced it, folding her fingers together in front of her like Mrs. Wilmert had taught her, she couldn't even remember the first word, or how to place the tone in her dia-frame like Mrs. Wilmert kept saying.

Fedalia couldn't answer Papa when she heard him call and call from the parlor, then the kitchen. She heard his footsteps hurrying through the house to the side bedroom. He found her standing behind the door.

"Fedalia! Papa's Fedalia-baby! What's the matter, sweetheart? What is it, baby?" She hid her face on his shoulder as he picked her up in his arms and carried her over to Mama's rocker, where he sat her down in his lap.

"There, there," he said for quite a long time.

"Papa—the recital and my white dress——"

"There, there, sweetheart—there'll be other recitals."

When Fedalia stared up at the blackness between her and the bedroom ceiling later that night, she heard, for the first time in her life, the courthouse clock strike every hour till dawn. Again and again she said over the things Papa had told her. It was something that happened to everyone—every girl, that is, so you could get to be a mother, but you must never let anybody know when it was happening.

Papa didn't say a single word about how you actually started a baby, so her guess was probably right, you do get a baby every time you sit on a boy's lap.

But then what was that about the Plague? You mustn't let a boy touch you. . . . I suppose that must also include your husband.

But then how could you ever sit on his lap and have a baby? And everybody sat on their father's lap. . . . It was pretty mixed up; only one thing was sure—she was certainly not going to let anybody kiss her—ever—not even Charlie.

CHAPTER SEVEN

During the next few years, as though pleased with the way Fedalia's rare combination of gold hair and brownish-blue, blue-brownish eyes had turned out, Nature proceeded to develop the rest of this girl with a lavish hand. Mr. Parker saw to it that there were no opportunities for Charlie or Shink Burns or any other of Fort Madison's young men to play Prince to his Sleeping Beauty. "No division of interest" was the road to Olympus, and Mrs. Wilmert the immediate password. Indeed Mrs. Wilmert's belief in her own divinity was growing rapidly under Mr. Parker's feverish enthusiasms, despite the fact that the first vocal lesson she had ever given in her life was to Fedalia.

"Now, my little bird, before you go we will practice *bel canto*. Every singer——"

"Excuse me, Mrs. Wilmert, I still don't understand what

that means." Fedalia was lying on her back on the floor of Mrs. Wilmert's "studio," a small pink and light blue parlor, chiefly occupied by a black upright piano, a canary cage, and a collapsible metal music stand. The metronome on the piano had ticked continuously throughout the lesson. Four heavy books were piled on Fedalia's stomach.

"My little bird. Everyone knows what bel canto means. You simply can't sing correctly without it. Up, up, up with the tone." Mrs. Wilmert wafted a small hand up, up, up. "Out, out, out with the tone, just like a bird."

"Mrs. Wilmert, the dictionary in the library says bel canto means 'beauty of sound.' How should I practice that?"

"Exactly, my little bird. Beauty of sound. Everything comes from the diaframe. Everything. Now, without toppling the books, pant for me, dear. Mouth open, tongue loose, ready —— Pant! That is right, two, three, four, just-like-a-puppy-dog pant! two, three, four, and faster, two, three, and faster, two, three, four, faster, faster, faster, a-a-and—stop, two, three. Fine, my little bird! Just fine, and that's enough for today. Upsadaisy." Fedalia removed the books and got to her feet.

"Now for the surprise, dear. The music store telephoned to say that 'Lo! Hear the Gentle Lark' came in from Chicago this morning! What do you say about that?"

"Really, Mrs. Wilmert? And can I try it over tonight? I'm sure I could pick it out on our piano. I'll stop over to the store right now and get it on the way home."

"They're going to leave it with your father over at the paper, dear."

"But he works late tonight, Mrs. Wilmert."

"He wanted you to go straight home from here, and it will be just as well to do your scales and Ick leeba Dick tonight, anyway. I'll walk with you to the bridge. Get your things, dear."

"Why, Mrs. Wilmert? It's such a long way for you to walk every time. And it's not even dark yet and I am past seventeen."

Mrs. Wilmert handed Fedalia her music roll. "Come, my little bird. We can memorize on the way and practice our breathing, shall we? It's important, you know."

Ernie and Jess set pins every Saturday night down at the bowling alley. Fedalia sent them off with a warm supper, did the dishes, and sat down with her darning basket. She had Charlie's last two valentines down at the bottom and took them out and read over the verses. She hadn't tried to see him alone, knowing Papa didn't want her to, and Charlie'd given up, too, since the night Papa had delivered her to the dance at the gym and then waited to take her home.

At school in the halls it was no use, either, with someone always around and poor Charlie so tongue-tied. One time she did go into the drugstore where he worked after school, but the counter was full of kids and their cherry Cokes and when she tried to talk to him he couldn't even look at her, let alone answer.

He was always at the church whenever she sang for any affair, though, even the grown-up sociables. There he always was, waiting around in the loggia or in the back of the lecture room when she knew he must have had to sneak away from the drugstore in order to be there listening.

Nobody seemed to call him Runt any more since the race, and he didn't seem short at all now, with his long pants instead of the knickerbockers his mother always used to make him wear buckled over his knees. Certain afternoons she could see his curly black head bent over the table in the chem lab, and several times she tried unsuccessfully to make him look up by staring hard. . . .

The footsteps on the front porch were so light she wasn't positive she heard them. The rapping was light, too, but now she knew there was somebody there.

She dropped the darning basket from her lap, getting up hurriedly to go to the door.

It was Charlie, pale with the moonlight that reflected into his face from the hall window, but wearing his turtle-neck sweater like a veteran returned to uniform for a vital emergency.

"I know they're not home and I had to come over. I . . . uh . . ." He had said all he could say.

"Charlie, come inside." Fedalia had left the hall light on the pilot when she answered the door. Charlie dropped down on the hall seat. Fedalia sat down next to him. The words unsaid for so long, came fast.

"Charlie, you were so wonderful the day you won the Letter, and I was so proud of you and I wanted to tell you for so long and we never saw each other without a million other kids around. That's what I came in the drugstore to tell you that day, remember, Charlie? And the kids were there and I was going to say it anyway, but you were so busy I couldn't get you to look at me."

"I can't look at you now."

"Why not, Charlie? I loved your valentines. Did you get mine? I meant what they said. Me, always rushing to Mrs. Wilmert and you having to be at the drugstore and Papa not wanting me to see anybody or go anyplace but to my music lessons. Of course he's right about a division of interest being weakening."

"I feel weak, all right."

"So do I. Charlie, look at me. I have to tell you . . ." Charlie raised his head, looking full into her face, dropped his eyes quickly, then raised them again to hers. Fedalia reached over to kiss his cheek.

It happened clumsily at first. Their inexperienced arms collided trying to find the way. If their lips could meet nothing would ever be as it had been again, Fedalia knew. She'd understand, even without knowing. All the breath seemed to leave her body as Charlie held her there with his arms tight around her.

Suddenly the hall light was bright and there was Papa saying terrible things. The world twisted and spun around. *Papa, you're wrong. You're wrong. Please, Papa. Not in front of Charlie.*

Papa kept on, and kept on. One of Fedalia's stockings had twisted loose, sliding down to her shoe top, as she finally got to her feet.

Out through the parlor she ran, into the kitchen, through the entry to the back yard. In the dark the clothesline snapped her head back, dropping her to the ground. The rope made a burning welt on her forehead, and the half-frozen slush left patches of clammy, cold wetness on her dress. She got up, slipped down again, but she kept on through all the back yards, trying desperately to get away from the terror that would surely seize her if she stopped. The Lutheran Church . . . the planing mill . . . the long dark oak-tree blocks and the viaduct, then the greenhouse looming black and silent on the hill. Through the big iron gates she half ran, half stumbled, past the small chapel and far down the icy cinder road to the very edge of the bushes. She sank down onto the ridge of earth where Mama was.

Papa hadn't said a word all the way back from the cemetery or even while he was pinning the flannel rag with the bacon grease around her neck. He'd just been sitting silently on her bed all this time.

Once more I'll hear the courthouse strike every hour,

Fedalia thought as she counted twelve. The springs of her bed creaked softly as Papa got up and tiptoed out of the room. *Papa thinks I'm asleep . . . Charlie . . . I have to see him tomorrow no matter what Papa says.* The door opened again, letting the light in on Papa coming back. She could see the money jar in his hand.

"Asleep, Sister?" he said, whispering at first.

"No, Papa."

"How much money was there in the New York jar last time you looked?"

"I think about ninety dollars, Papa. Why?"

"Count it again, sweetheart." He handed her the big preserves jar that had started its banking career so long ago with Mama and the lettuce garden. Together they emptied out the same familiar stream of silver, but now there were bills too!

"Papa! Where did all this come from?"

Papa put the money back in the jar and stood up. "I'm afraid I held out on you kids about workin' late down at the paper Saturday and Sunday nights. Monroe's been feelin' poorly for some little while. Don't forget, he's been janitorin' down there since before any of you were born. Well, I been giving him a lift down there Saturdays and Sundays. I didn't want his money, but he's got a lot of pride. So he'd have had his feelin's hurt if I'd refused. Only four-bits here and six-bits there, but in time that counts up. Fedalia, there's one hundred dollars there in that jar that you young ones didn't know anything about! Enough to clean up the back piano payments and Mr. Garvey besides, and nearly sixty dollars toward the New York trip! And what do we need a piano for now, anyway, when the musician of the family goes to New York? Ever think of that, Fee? If we can get a good price from Mr. Vance, we got enough here for your fare and enough over with the piano money so's I think, come fall, we might chance it, Sister." Papa reached over to pat her head. She felt tears coming and buried her face in the pillow. Papa patted her for a while longer. When she lifted her head it was dark again and Papa was gone.

The courthouse clock struck once more.

CHAPTER EIGHT

"The letter's here from New Jersey! The letter's here
from New Jersey!" Ernie screamed through the house
and into the bedroom, trailing in freshly mowed grass. Fedalia
put down her darning basket and grabbed for the letter.

"Why, Ernie! It's written on a typewriter! Aunt Bernette
can't type on a typewriter, can she?"

"Judas H. Priest! Lookie that!"

"Ernest Parker, where did you pick up that terrible language? Oh gosh, it's only four o'clock, how can we wait till
Papa gets home?"

"Open it, Fee, open it! Judas H.—— Criminy, Papa
wouldn't care if you opened it."

"No, I shouldn't open it, but I can't wait till supper, I
know that. Ernie, I'm going to run down to the paper with
it."

"I'd go with you if I didn't have to finish Fletcher's dang
lawn. Hurry, now, will you, Fee?"

"You bet I will. Good-by, Ernie, while I change."

Ernie crashed out the door and exploded out the front and down the porch steps, slamming the bedroom door, the front door, and the screen door.

Aunt Bernette must have answered by return mail! That could mean she'd be glad for her to stay with them. The sooner she got down to the paper, the sooner she'd know.

She tied her black Peter-Thompson tie, running down the stairs, out the front door, and down the porch steps, realizing with a wave at Ernie across the street that she, too, had slammed the bedroom door, the front door, and the screen door.

She always sang her way places, particularly when she was in a hurry. It seemed to make the distance pass quicker. It took exactly two choruses of "Yes, We Have No Bananas" to get up to the Baptist Church and then two of "Rose of the Rio Grande" to the thread store. That was practically next door to the paper.

As long as she was singing in her head like that, she might as well be practicing "The Last Rose of Summer" for her lesson, excepting you certainly couldn't walk along fast in rhythm to that kind of a song. Rose of the Ri- o Grande— Rose of the Bor-der Land—One word then hand in hand— We'll leave the preacher's side room—Hap-py lit-tle bride and bride-groom, Ov-er those—"Hod-a-do, Mrs. Sutlough"— hills of sand—I've got our love nest planned—You claim it I'll name it Rose of Ri- o Grande . . . Rose of the Ri-o Grande . . . Rose of the Bor-der Land . . . One word then hand in hand—We'll leave the preacher's side room—Hap-py lit-tle—— "Charlie!"

"Hello, Fee. Where y' goin'?"

"To see Papa at the paper. Where you going, Charlie?"

"Oh . . . ah . . . no-place . . . I . . ."

Fedalia was always hoping to run into Charlie. It seemed

so strange not to run into him oftener in such a small town as Fort Madison. Then the few times they did run into each other, she was surer than ever that it wasn't safe to see him at all. They could never get to talking, someway. . . . Like now, the longer neither of them said anything, the harder it was to break the silence.

"Well, here's my corner, Charlie. I have to show this letter to Papa. Well . . . Good-by, Charlie. Glad to've run——"

"Glad to've run in——" They both said it at the same time. Fedalia stood for a moment, then turned slowly into the paper office, saying, "Good-by, Charlie."

She went down the steps to the little door and out through into the back and the clackety racket. Papa was ink all over his face. "Watchya got there, Sister?" he yelled over the clatter of the machines.

"Aunt Bernette's letter came this afternoon, Papa. I couldn't wait."

"Well, good! Let's open 'er up." Fedalia tore open the letter.

"It's typewritten, Papa," she said, handing Papa the pages. "Well, what do you know . . .

"*Dear Mr. Parker, or should I address you as Luther . . .*

"This is from her husband, Fee.

"*My wife has not been well for some months and has asked me to take care of this letter, which I am glad to do. Her ailment is not the point of this missive, but I will comment that it appears to be an unusual sickness, and stubborn. Your young daughter Fedalia will be welcome to stay in our small and very modest home, which is not much more than an hour and a half away from New York City, in answer to your query. That includes the trolley and ferry. Whatever she might care to pay will be acceptable, depending, of course, upon any* meals which she may take with us. You state that your plans for her embrace the fall, by which time Bernette may be improved. By all means, plan on Fedalia's coming. Answering your question about financing the trip, she should have a hundred dollars with her, at the very least, when she arrives, to take care of her expenses. As gifted as she unquestionably is, it will be some little time before she can establish sufficiently good connections to insure her earning any regular fees. One hundred fifty would be safer. I am sorry that I have never had the opportunity of meeting you or any of Bernette's people, but perhaps your daughter may start the forging of that neglected link. Bernette adds her love to my respectful greeting.

Sincerely,
George Broder

"Well, I *do* know. Criminy, he's pretty scissor-tail coat about it all, huh? Didn't dream Bernette hooked onto such a classy-sounding—— Well, we've got the hundred. We'll sew that right into your underwear when the time comes, and as soon as we get thirty dollars more, besides what's left in the jar, we can set the date and order the ticket! Now scat, Sister, and start supper. I'll be home in an hour. Here, take the letter. We'll talk it over tonight. Looks fine, doesn't it?"

"Sounds fine, Papa."

"Real high-class Eastern relatives . . ." Papa threw her a kiss. " 'By, sweetheart. Go straight home."

" 'By, Papa. You always say that. Now where else would I go? 'By."

CHAPTER NINE

The train slowly rumbled out of the station. Papa stood on the baggage truck, in full view of the assembled Fort Madisonians, waving his arms and yelling out, "Wave, everybody. There she goes!" Fedalia remembered seeing Mr. Vance and Farmer Garvey in the light of the sign over the lunchroom door. Ernie and Jess had given her train letters to read before dashing to the telegraph pole at the end of the station to be the last to wave. Mrs. Wilmert and some of the kids from her class gathered around as the train started to move. They were singing "Barney Google," only with different words.

"Our Fedalia, with her good, good, googily voice.
Our Fedalia, she is bound to win the prize.
Till she comes from far away
We will think of her alway,
Our Fedalia, with her good, good, googily VOICE."

The train seemed to go slow, but it was already passing along the dark factories. What a very short time between being in that big crowd at the station and being more entirely alone than she had ever been in her life.

She went back into the train and sat on the edge of the little bed with the green curtains, wondering about the hammock next to the window. Fran Cook had loaned her the shiny brown grip for her nightgown and other things for the trip so she wouldn't have to be unstrapping the telescope suitcase. She slipped inside the curtains and found the big buttons that fastened the curtains together.

Going away from Papa and the boys and home, maybe forever. Her lonesomeness was solid and quiet.

She never had felt her eyes so wide open as she lay there with her knees bent over the brown grip at the foot. She'd get her dress all wrinkled. And Mr. Quimby's bouquet! She reached down to her feet for it and banged her head almost too hard not to cry out. She could think things out simply and clearly if she could only side-step that stony lonesomeness. She might go on being scared and lonesome for a while, but being scared has nothing to do with being a coward, and there is always a straight simple answer to everything. . . . But why didn't Charlie come down to the depot to say good-by to her?

So many clanging bells ringing in the dark night, and speeding lights whirling by, flashing through the crack between the shade and the window sill.

Just think of Mr. Gale giving Papa the twenty dollars down at the drugstore! All day Papa had said not to worry about what they needed to make up the money for the ticket, but when Farmer Garvey had turned Papa down, Fedalia was almost ready to give up the whole trip. Either that or take it out of the money sewed into her underwear. But Papa'd insisted, "Uncle George said that's the very least you'll need, and Uncle George knows. We will *not* touch that hundred dollars." And then he thought of Mr. Gale down at the drugstore. Mr. Gale, of all people. Cross old Mr. Gale with his camphor and his pills and his white coat. But Papa seemed so sure, and the way he'd pounded up the porch steps tonight coming home from the paper, Fedalia knew he had the money even before he burst in with the two ten-dollar bills in his hand. And here she was on the train!

It was so nice of Mr. Quimby to drive them to the depot. Fedalia blushed in the dark, thinking over the conversation Papa and Mr. Quimby had had while she was wrapping up the chicken for her shoe-box lunch. They'd thought she couldn't hear them because Mr. Quimby had said he couldn't understand "about Fedalia giving the young men such a cold shoulder. Why, she could have left busted hearts all over this county. Never saw such a beautiful child nor such an all-fired desirable young woman. And Fedalia just never gave anybody a look-in." Papa's voice answered Mr. Quimby. "Her career came first with Fedalia. A division of interest is weakening, I used to always tell her. And she understood that. And b'time this house was tended to, she was right on her lessons, doing just what Mrs. Wilmert told her over and over, every day—conscientious and real determined."

"You know, she's got a pretty tough row to hoe." That was Mr. Quimby again. "Back there all alone in New York. She's bound to find out a lot a' things the hard way, knowing no more than she does about things."

"Don't worry about that, Mr. Quimby. I had several very plain talks with her on the subject."

"Well, that's good. In any case, it'll take a lot of courage for an inexperienced girl like Fedalia to hold her own, back there in the biggest city in the world. A lot of real courage."

"She's got a lot of real courage, Mr. Quimby. We'll certainly miss that girl around this house. She always set the boys a good example. Picked up after 'um but never spoiled 'um exactly. She'd first make up her mind about what was right. Then she'd go about gettin' it done. Set me a good example, too, when hard things had to be done—like quittin' smoking." She knew Papa's eyes would be wandering over to the mantel.

"Why don't you throw those pipes out, Red? You're only stringing the agony, having them right there where you can see them all the time."

"Oh, I couldn't do that, Mr. Quimby. They're like old friends. They've helped me through a lot of problems the past forty years. Look at this old black one. Fits my jaw just like my hat fits my head. Always smoked that one in the evenin', readin' aloud to the kids. See there? That's one of Jess's tooth marks. Fedalia had the measles and Mama was havin' Ernie and I was helpin' Jess to teethe. Smoked that corncob during the day and the amber one at home Sundays. Took twenty years to cloudy her up dark that way."

"And Doc McKewen said quit—just like that?"

"That's the way he said it. Makes you wonder. If I'd quit twenty years ago, it wouldn't have been hard, but on the other hand, look at all the comfort I've had out of those pipes. Still, look at me now—can't get them out of my mind for even a minute."

"Maybe old Doc'll relent in a couple a' months."

"I guess not. He said, 'No more smoking—ever'—pretty emphatic. Feda-a-l-ia . . . Si-i-ister. Time we were getting on to the depot."

The train was sliding along evenly now, or else she was getting used to the motion.

Papa would be walking home with Mr. Vance and Farmer Garvey. They'd be crossing the bridge by now—past the flats —there'd be the one quiet light over the Lutheran Church door. Mrs. Sutlough would be sitting on her porch steps in the dark as they passed by; they'd pretend not to see her. It wasn't polite to speak to somebody there in the dark who liked to sit alone like that. The boys would have gone on ahead, prob'ly up to the soda grill. Papa'd be going up their steps now and into the house alone. It would be awfully hard on Papa going into the house alone. She tried to go in with him, thinking it as strongly as she could, so he'd know she'd followed him all the way home like that in her mind. It would be so strange without one of them yelling or singing around. The clock would tick extra-loud.

She felt the train pulling her along, and yet she seemed to be dreaming now. She was right there looking at Papa, even hearing his thoughts, like he was saying them, only he wasn't exactly talking. Or was he? She could see him looking up at the mantel.

"I've done my best with the kids. At least they've never got into any trouble—brought home respectable reports from school through the years—except Ernie's red F in Chemistry. Never had a letter from any of the kids. None of 'em ever been away from home before. I hope Fedalia will write about everything so I can imagine her comings and goings."

"I'll write, Papa," she said out loud, but Papa didn't seem to hear her. He picked up his black pipe and went slowly into the kitchen. The kitchen stool was wobbling a bit lately.

"Maybe Jess can put a couple nails in that stool when he gets home from the paper Saturday afternoon. Mr. Graves told me Jess is going to do fine in the newspaper business. How many times I've talked things over with the boys right here on this kitchen stool, cutting their hair when they were little."

"I'll write, Papa," she said again.

Papa went over to the kitchen table and pulled the drawer open. "I wonder where my barber shears are. What a big day that was when the hand clippers came in the mail from

Sears and Roebuck. Fedalia wanted her hair cut too. 'Now, Sister, you don't use clippers on girls.' " Fedalia heard Papa rummaging around in the drawer. He closed it—walked back over to the stool. "Mama was here then. I always said she gave the kids such a good start that my job hasn't been hard at all. Mama sure had courage. . . ." Papa staggered against the stool, and the stem of the black pipe snapped and dropped noisily onto the kitchen floor.

Papa! The train stopped so suddenly that it banged and shuddered. Fedalia's eyes opened wide again. Her heart pounded and the train stood so silently she was afraid to move or hardly breathe.

Fedalia was surprised next morning to find the Chicago station so dirty and so old. There were such crowds of people hurrying by and making so much noise. Sitting in her own corner of the hard bench with her telescope suitcase under her knees and the brown grip on her lap and the shoe box under her arm, she felt quite safe, though. She wasn't any part of this and she wasn't afraid. Whoever heard of the actors walking down off the stage and involving the audience in the play?

She hadn't been able to forget the vividness of her dream on the train last night. It had seemed to happen as though her eyes were open the whole time. Of course she had never had a dream of any kind on a train before.

The time seemed to pass very slowly, but still it surprised her when she heard them call out her train.

The Erie train was like the Santa Fe, except the floor of the Pullman car was exposed wood without a carpet, and you stepped down a little from the door into the car itself. There weren't many people in the train, but just the same she put her telescope under the seat and kept the brown grip on her lap because she could see that only part of this seat belonged to her and she might as well learn to be comfortable with the part she was entitled to, then if some other people got on at some other station who were entitled to sit here in part of this seat, she would be just as comfortable as ever with no adjustment at all to make.

Her shoe box was tucked in next to the window, and she thought she'd better eat something. Papa had fried way too much chicken. She knew she had to try to stop worrying about Papa because there was no way she could get a message either to or from Papa here, rolling across the United States in a train. I hope Papa's all right . . . I hope Papa's all right . . . I hope Papa's all right . . .

CHAPTER TEN

She had been all tidied and packed up, ready to leave
the train, nearly an hour before they got to Newark.
It was exciting how the train glided right in even with the
platform. Now then, Papa had said she should go to the
waiting room and Uncle George was to look for her there.

The telegraph boys were yelling loud over the crashing,
bustling noises. "Teleegrams to all pernts" is what it sounded
like, nasal and high-pitched and strange. She was glad she
had given the shoe box to the porter, partly because he
seemed so surprised at her generosity and partly because she
had her hands full carrying the telescope and the brown grip
down the stairs and through the tunnel up into the station
and the waiting room. "Over by the ladies' retiring room,"
Papa had said in the letter to Uncle George. Well! There it
was, the sign saying LADIES, over in the far corner.

Should she kiss Uncle George? Should she even call him

Uncle George? He had written the letter so carefully, calling Papa "Mr. Parker, or should I say Luther?" And signing it "George Broder." She certainly felt as though she should kiss Aunt Bernette if she came with him. She felt nervousness all through her veins and her stomach. She'd felt that way yesterday as the train was coming into Chicago. Come to think of it, she used to feel that way when she was little, when the streetcar arrived at their stop coming home from the fairgrounds back in Fort Madison. That nervous feeling was probably part of traveling from one place to another.

"Pardon me, Fedalia?"

It was wonderful hearing her own name! Way, way away here in this New Jersey depot!

"Uncle—Broder! I mean——" She felt she should kiss him after such a disrespectful mistake and put down the baggage quickly. His calmness stood out in front of him, however, like a wide counter. She knew she couldn't gracefully reach over it, so she just said, "I didn't know whether you wanted me to kiss you, like a good many nieces do their uncles, or even whether you wanted me to address you as Uncle George or Mr. Broder or which would be the proper thing."

The gentleman made no attempt to break in on her explanation, hearing it out like it was a recitation. When Fedalia finished, he smiled in a straight line without opening his lips at all, removed his small brown hat, and said, "Uncle George, by all manner of means." He had a pair of gloves in his hand and a brown kind of light overcoat, hooked invisibly, straight down the middle, almost to the bottom. She noticed he had small feet in keeping with his small, rather sharp features and his rather short size, but not in proportion when you realized that he was—well—thick, almost like Mr. Novcheck, the blacksmith at home. He said, "Your aunt Bernette, as you may have expected, could not come to meet you. She sends her regrets—from the hospital, as an absolute matter of fact."

"I'm so sorry, Uncle George. I hope she——"

"I'm afraid nothing can be done for her. There is a bus that we are to take, just down those stairs, there, and down at the corner. I can manage these things of yours. Now . . . Fedalia . . ." They started down the steps.

"Yes, Uncle George?"

"You and your father were very close?"

Papa? Why should he ask about Papa? "Papa? I don't know what you mean."

"I have heard from your home, Fedalia—by telegraph. . . . I think we might wait till we find seats on the bus. You know?" They had just stepped outside the station and Uncle George stopped and turned so he could look directly at Fedalia.

Papa! "Uncle George, what is it? Did Papa telegraph or what, please, Uncle George?"

He looked at her mouth, followed her words carefully as she said them, like reading lips. "Now, now, Fedalia. The bus will be here soon and I prefer not to say any more till I have you inside, sitting down, you know?"

Fedalia looked up and down the noisy crowded street. A bus drew up and stopped. "It has a self-folding door," she explained to herself, trying to keep frantically occupied with something.

They found a seat with a rack above for her brown grip and telescope. Then Uncle George said, "Your father is dead, Fedalia."

CHAPTER ELEVEN

It was like Papa had lived his whole life just for one thing—getting her to New York. And when that was accomplished he didn't have to worry any more, about late nights at the paper or anything else.

Uncle George knew she'd be crying and it was nice of him to stay on the porch. She wasn't crying, though. Her eyes felt wide open as she sat in the silence of Uncle George's parlor.

Maybe Uncle George was kind and understanding in the way he tried to break the news. Not wanting to tell her till she was sitting down in the bus must have been his way of being kind. It had frightened her at first, his looking so closely at her—studying her face, and then dropping his eyes the moment she looked at him.

After Uncle George had said what he said about Papa being gone, Fedalia realized how the strange dream on the train had fastened onto her the whole trip as being true. This had cushioned the shock of Uncle George's words. Uncle George must have been worried trying to figure out how to tell her. *I knew it already, Uncle George.* Maybe she should tell him that.

They had walked to Uncle George's house from the bus, and here she was in West Guage, New Jersey, in a house that felt a great deal like Fort Madison, Iowa.

What would Ernie and Jess do about the funeral and who would look after their meals? Mrs. Sutlough's Elvirah could come in and cook part time and they'd eat downtown now and then, but where would the money come from with Papa's paper wages gone? Her place was home with the boys. She ought to take what was left and go home, but she couldn't do that at all when Papa'd done all he'd done to get her here.

She didn't know very much about hysteria, but she knew she'd been thinking all these things rapidly, one right after the other, quickly, because she felt like she would give in to the sobbing if she let her mind slow down. She knew now why she fought against giving in to it. Papa wasn't really dead till she mourned him with all the grief that was bursting in her, and she had to keep Papa alive till he could see those magic glittering New York walls through her eyes.

"Uncle George." The small window in the parlor was open onto the porch.

"Yes, Fedalia?" Uncle George came in through the front door. The breeze tinkled the glass wind bells hanging in the hall. Fedalia's heart seemed to stop for a second as a terrified hissing came from somewhere just behind her chair—from a small cat crowding back into its box, arching and spitting.

"Your aunt Bernette's kitten. Stop your spitting, Raggy. I—have to keep that cord around her neck to make sure she doesn't slip outdoors. You know how quick they are."

"Yes, Uncle George," Fedalia said.

Uncle George looked at Fedalia and then away. "I will dispose of the poor thing one day soon, humanely, of course. But thus far I've been just putting it off." Uncle George looked down at his small shoes.

"Uncle George, how far is it to New York? Just to see it, I mean."

"It's less than an hour to Hoboken by bus, if that's what you're thinking of. The entire New York sky line is, of course, visible from there."

"Could you please show me how to get that bus, please, Uncle George? I have to go to Hoboken right now."

If Uncle George had told her where she should get off the bus, she'd forgotten, so Fedalia just stayed on till the man called out, "Hoboken Bus Terminal." Then she followed the people out to the street. This was so near to New York that she ought to be seeing it any minute, around some corner, past some building or down some street.

How could such plain dark gray and brown iron and stones blot out a great city like New York, blot it out so completely from sight that she had to hunt for it behind a fish store with cracked white enamel trays in the window, embedded in an old ugly red brick square pile?

There were other red brick piles just like it on both sides of the street all the way to the corner, even down into the next block, dangling rusty fire escapes and advertising signs, small advertising signs fitted under the steps leading up to the second story, or maybe it was the first story, because the ground-floor story seemed to start under those steps, more like a basement. And there were big tailor signs and dressmaker signs across the front, all the way to the tops of the buildings. Fish piled up in one store, broken furniture piled up in another—everything old and noisy and dirty—old and hopeless.

But then Mr. Novchek's blacksmith shop back in Fort

Madison was probably very hopeless-looking to somebody seeing it for the first time, too—still, Mr. Novchek was so proud of it he gave that big party to everybody on the block the day he paid off his mortgage, everybody roasting weenies right there in the forge. Maybe Mr. S-h-r-e-e-c-k-i-n-g-e-i-s-t here in Hoboken is exactly that proud of his fish store.

Fedalia crossed over to the downhill side and after she reached the corner, clear of parked trucks for a moment, there was the river. The Hudson River! In another half block she had an unbroken view of the other side of it, the New York side! Great buildings began to show among the trees and the green along the far bank. Papa had thought New York was mostly cement and bricks without any trees.

She lost her view now for a while, being close to the final row of buildings between her and the river, factories with tracks and freight cars in the way. If she could get past those boxcars the river should be visible again and the whole New York view along with it. She saw how wrinkled her train dress was as she climbed over the coupling between the boxcars. She was getting the skirt rusty too. Oh, Papa! Look! Look, Papa! Look! Way down *there*, look! Those *castles* and *forts* and *palaces* all the way down at the end of the river, wreathed in clouds . . . I'm *here*, Papa! In New York!

CHAPTER TWELVE

Boxcars are the same every place, Hoboken or Fort
Madison. It helped, someway, to lean on that boxcar
until the crying gradually stopped. Papa's gone forever, Papa's
gone forever . . . But she was only saying over words that
wouldn't penetrate as a fact at all, so after a while she stopped
trying and remembered, instead, the way he looked in his
overcoat with the velvet collar, proudly taking them all to
the library when they were too little to go alone. Or in his
gray sweater with the elbow patches, striding along with the
lawn mower summer evenings, laughing at the boys and their
grass fights, even stuffing handfuls of grass down their necks
himself . . . Then waving good-by from the baggage truck
down at the Santa Fe depot. Papa was right, it was a goal
of a lifetime just to get to this beautiful city from a small
faraway Iowa town. It looked quiet and dignified from here,
even restful. The boats seemed to move so slowly and the

smoke almost hung in the air till it could be either smoke or clouds.

Those buildings must be high enough to be reaching right up into the clouds. How all that slow majesty would tower over her when she moved herself into that city, shining now in the last of the Hoboken sunset. A thing can tower over you so big it sometimes disappears from your view. She'd find out about its dignity and its towering majesty and its faraway calmness, and whatever came, she'd be ready.

She felt calm about Papa now.

It was nearly dark. She realized she'd better try to find the way back to the bus station. A little dirty-white dog came wiggling up. She put down her hand for it to smell, like Papa always told her. The dog smelled her hand and licked it. Dogs recognize friendly people by their smell; cats do too.

Funny that Raggy was so afraid of Uncle George.

Uncle George was standing right by the bus as she got off. "Uncle George!"

"I was just beginning to worry about you, Fedalia." He took her arm carefully, just touching her elbow till she stepped up over the curb onto the sidewalk. Then he moved over to the street side of her and took his hand away.

"I'm sorry I was so long," she said. "I didn't think you'd be waiting. . . ."

"It would be easy for you to become confused in a strange place," Uncle George said. "I didn't mind the waiting, although I underestimated your return by fifty minutes or so." She saw his silent smile again. "We will take something in the cafeteria in the next block. It is not at all fancy, but a very dependable eating place."

"I don't eat much for supper, Uncle George, generally."

Uncle George looked at her. "It's called 'dinner' in the

East. Supper is, for us, an extra meal before retiring, if the occasion demands, and your heavy Middle West dinners at noon are more often salads or sandwiches here, which we call 'luncheon.' "

She felt his hand on her elbow again and they turned into a small store with enamel around the window like the Hoboken fish store. There was a cafeteria in Fort Madison, so she knew about getting the tray and the silver rolled up in a napkin, and that you had to come back to fill your thick tumbler with water after you had put your food down on the table. She took meat loaf and Jello and mashed potatoes and a roll, because Uncle George did. There wasn't anything to say while they ate. Uncle George paid both slips on the way out.

Uncle George's street was dark and she was very glad he had met her at the bus, because she never would have been able to pick out the small, completely vine-covered house set deep away from the street in the long, empty block.

He took her elbow as they turned into the walk, touching it till they'd gone up the porch steps. He took a key out of his vest pocket and opened the door. She could hear Raggy's frightened hiss as the door closed behind them, and there was a moment or so of pitch dark as Uncle George felt along the wall for the switch. It made a small singing sound like the switch at the head of the cellar steps in Sutlough's house.

"Do you have your nightdress and things you will need for bed in the one grip?" He was bending over her things there in the hall. "Or will you require the large case as well?" The bulb in the hall had no shade over it, but it was not at all bright or cheerful.

"I could just rest on a couch or anyplace, Uncle George," Fedalia said hurriedly. "I'm sure I've been a great deal of trouble, and you must have had things to do while I've been taking up your time. . . ."

72

"As long as I am solely responsible for your well-being, Fedalia, I will endeavor to accept that responsibility to the hilt." He rushed into his last word, biting "hilt" off sharp and short, with a jerk of his head. She looked quickly at him as he straightened up with the brown grip in his hand. He was smiling with his lips open for the first time. His teeth were small and gray-colored and even.

"I need both, Uncle George. I can carry them just fine. . . ." She picked up the telescope.

"Let me have the large case, Fedalia." He went to the door and opened it.

"Where are we going, Uncle George?"

"My dear niece, you didn't expect to stay under this roof with your Aunt Bernette—away? That would never do, even though I am a relative by virtue of having married your mother's sister. Propriety, my dear. There is a quiet and very respectable rooming house at the head of the street. Miss Broder is the landlady."

"Miss Broder?"

"My sister, Fedalia. And may I impress upon you that she is to know nothing of your identity?"

"I don't understand, Uncle George."

"My sister and I were inseparable till your Aunt Bernette took sick. After that her attitude was such that I could only conclude she would actually welcome my wife's continued illness. Some deep-seated jealousy she had kept hidden from me. Needless to say, I have permitted no semblance of cordial relations to resume. And I have no wish that they be resumed through you. You will put in your appearance merely as a Miss Parker desirous of renting a room as advertised on the card in her window. Do you understand, Fedalia?"

"Why—yes, Uncle George."

He put down the telescope suitcase, looked at her sharply,

then away. In the hall mirror on the wall she saw his upper lip tighten over the short gray teeth.

"On second thought," he said, "I'm sure she watches this house constantly. She has no doubt already seen you entering or leaving."

"Uncle George, I would much prefer to tell Miss Broder the truth——"

"Now, now, now. Later, of course. But for the present I'm sure it would be wiser not to vouchsafe our relationship. Of course, if by any curious chance she should ask you——"

"I will certainly tell her."

"I'm sure of it, dear niece." His odd little forward bow accompanied the remark. "For now," he continued, "just say you are a young lady who expects to be of some part-time help to me in New York. Errands and the like? It will be no deviation from actuality, considering that I fully intend to ask you to make certain purchases for me in the city. From time to time?" He picked up the case once more and indicated the door with a polite gesture of his head.

"What kind of purchases, Uncle George?" Fedalia said. She stepped out onto the porch.

"Certain—ah—materials I require in my—ah—psychological experiments. Fascinating phenomena into which I shall initiate you—in time. You know?" He touched her elbow. "We will require a privacy that my sister might try to prevent if she suspected our relationship. I mean our relationship as uncle and niece. How much more jealous she would surely be of an attractive young niece than of a middle-aged wife. You know?"

He guided her down the steps, down the full length of dark walk, till they turned up the block. Then he crossed over to the street side of her and dropped his hand. "I will walk with you as far as discretion permits." When they reached the corner he stopped.

"The house is just there. Next to the corner across the street. I'm sorry not to help you all the way with your luggage." He handed her the telescope. "Will you take breakfast with me in the morning?"

"Thank you, Uncle George. I will be leaving very early for New York. But I'll stop by on the way back, if that's all right," she added hurriedly.

"By all manner of means. I expect you to. Good night, Fedalia." He raised his small brown hat.

"Good night, Uncle George, and thank you ever so much. I'd like awfully to visit Aunt Bernette at the hospital if it would be all right."

"We'll see," he said, turning back the way they had come.

The only light in the next block was shining rather feebly from the parlor window of the second house from the corner, showing a handwritten ROOMS FOR RENT sign. Fedalia was glad to put the bags down on the porch. The bell was in the center of the door, and it rang loudly in and out as she pressed and released the button. She had to press it a second time before the light in the hall came on and a middle-aged woman with a very tired and noticeably unsmiling face opened the door. She had a wrapper pulled around her, and some very blond hair was not quite concealed under her dust cap.

"Well?" the lady said through the narrow opening she had provided by barely permitting the door to stand ajar.

"Miss Broder?"

"How did you know my name?"

Fedalia swallowed. "Why—I——"

"Were you looking for a room?"

"Yes, ma'am. Just temporarily——"

"Temporarily is all the way I rent 'em. Eight dollars for one week."

"That will be fine. I'm Miss Parker——

Miss Broder pushed the door shut and disappeared. In a few moments she returned wearing a heavy cloth coat. She opened the door, pushed the latch, stepped out onto the porch, closing the door behind her. "This way," she said, stepping down off the porch and leading the way around the side of the house. A clicking sound released a beam of light from the small flashlight in her hand. Fedalia could see that the house had been made over with separate partitions and entrances.

"There's a room up them steps. Top floor." Miss Broder flashed the light up the side of the house where a thin outside stairway made out of metal pipe climbed up through the vines to a small landing and doorway just under the roof. "It locks on the inside. Bathroom's down here through that door with the light on all night. You got your separate entrance and I got mine, so no reason for you to bother me or me you. Eight dollars in advance. You can leave it on the commode tonight if you decide to stay after seeing the room. I'll hold the light on the steps, then I'm going to bed. You can find your way down if you don't like the room."

Fedalia said, "Thank you, Miss Broder," starting up the stairway, trying as carefully as possible not to bang each step with the telescope in front or the brown bag behind. "I'll stay tonight, anyhow. It's really too late to go anywhere else. Not that I'm not sure the room won't be fine and all. . . ." She reached the landing and looked back just as the flashlight below her went out. "Good night," she called down into the dark, but there was no answer.

CHAPTER THIRTEEN

In the morning sunlight the big red ferryboat coming into Jersey seemed to be moving slowly enough, Fedalia thought, but by the time its awkward front hit against the line of poles, it appeared to be coming in much too fast, bending the poles back with a series of great protesting squeaks. Some two feet from the edge, however, it miraculously slowed down as a heavy foamy churning underneath held the movement back till the boat's front rim fitted smoothly and exactly into the curved edge of the wharf.

In a second the man on the boat dropped two ropes around two piles and unfastened the chain across the front. Then all the silent watching people on the boat began chattering and moving, no longer silent, banging their feet down on the heavy metal hood that connected boat and shore.

So many new, new things. Her first ocean—way off there in the haze, her first river, even her first boat! And promising

so much, the tall spires . . . the skyscrapers standing so still
. . . just waiting off there, far down the river.

The gulls flapped and cried all around the boat. The smells
became different, and the small-size rattly-bang, high-pitched
noises of the rapidly fading streets and the pier became
hollow, distant sounds now, not sharp or edgy or clattery, but
calm and thick and open and full of echoes. That smell was
salt, of course—that sea smell.

She didn't do much thinking as they moved out into the
water. She just let the strange sounds and sights and smells
happen all around her. The big thin spires seemed to turn
away a little at a time as the smaller factories and wharves
directly across started to appear bigger and clearer in the
foreground. . . .

New York was one thing, glittering from far away, a group
of quiet, friendly, magic towers, but this close-at-hand dirty,
cold-looking collection of bleak windows, chimneys, and water
tanks was quite another. How would she know where to find
someone interested in a singer? After leaving eight dollars
last night at the rooming house she had ninety dollars—well,
about eighty-eight now—pinned to her underwear, and of
course she'd have to start making something before spending too much of it. It should be like a fund to go home with
in an emergency, Papa said. There would never be any emergency now, though. What could happen worse than Papa
dying? And if she didn't go home for that, she certainly
would never go home till she'd won the success like Papa
wanted.

The people crowded to the front of the ferryboat as it
started turning in toward the landing pier. Everyone quieted
down again as the posts squeaked submissively while the boat
nosed right into New York City.

It was noisy and dirty and crowded with rushing, frantic
people. As she was hurried along in the dingy ferry shed and

out into the grimy street Fedalia felt the greatness of the city flowing through everything around her, giving its special quality to the people and the sounds and the air.

Uncle George didn't know anything at all about the music world, he said. He had mentioned his office in West Guage, saying he rarely had any reason even to go to New York. He had said also he thought the best place for her to look around and to inquire would be on Broadway near Times Square, where so many theaters were. Always ask a policeman, he told her. Papa had said that, too, so she would just hurry along as fast as possible, like all these other people, looking for a policeman.

By the time she got to Broadway and was walking along it in crowds that were so thick you couldn't even take a full step, she had discovered that men sold the newspapers instead of boys, that boys pushed racks of dresses along, right out in the middle of the street, that the elevated trains had to be boarded from one side of the street if you wanted to go uptown and from the other side for downtown, that the only directions were "up," "down," or "cross-town," and that besides its wild assortment of racket and din, this city had a constant background of awesome, toneless sound that followed you wherever you went.

Contributing to this characteristic giant murmur was a man with a high fur hat, dressed like one of the "six hundred" in the steel-engraving pictures at the Fort Madison library. He looked at least seven feet tall in this hat and kept telling everyone who passed by that there was "immediate seating in the balcony."

Fedalia edged back of the giant general over to the ticket window, where a flashing young lady with long earrings and lipstick crossed her legs on a high stool. The gold machine ground out a ticket.

79

"I didn't want to go to the show," Fedalia said, "I only wanted to ask——"

"Balcony only. Forty cents, pleeuz."

"Thank you, I didn't want to go to the——"

"Balcony only, madam. I c'n hear um saynit clear in heeyuh. That's the idear of um been out thaayuh. Forty cents, madam—Pleeuz."

"I only want to ask if they need any singers here."

"Any sing-gers? Madam, I don't own this playus. I merely sell the tickets. I don't even know the man who owns this playus or the man who knows the man who knows the man who hires the sing-gers, even. Now I punched out your ticket and I cayunt punch it back in. That's forty cents, madam, for the balcony ticket. Pleeeuz."

"I didn't ask for the ticket, miss, and I cannot afford the time or money to go to the show just now. I'm very sorry."

What's right is right. Fedalia looked through the glass, right in the young lady's eye. "Good-by."

I guess that's not the place to ask for a job in the show business, Fedalia thought as she walked away. *I know I'll have to go to the people back on the stage sooner or later, and there's no use putting it off.* There didn't seem to be any way of going around the block to find the stage entrance, and there wasn't anything logical about its location when she finally did find it, twenty minutes later, down a narrow alley right beside the theater lobby, not ten feet from the ticket window.

She stood for a few moments at the end of the alley, looking at a sign on the door which read: STAGE ENTRANCE —POSITIVELY NO ADMITTANCE—THIS MEANS YOU!!! Walking through a sign like that took some thinking over, at least.

While she was thinking, a boy with a cigarette and a small black dog came hurrying along, holding a loud conversation with a young fellow partly hidden behind a bundle of laundry. Their conversation broke off abruptly as they reached Fedalia. Their eyes quickly dropped to her ankles and slowly back up again. "She can't be real," the boy with the dog gasped, dropping his cigarette and reaching behind him in a mock daze for the doorknob. The older boy followed through the door.

Fedalia also took hold of the doorknob and walked in.

CHAPTER FOURTEEN

The most surprising contrast to the rolling mountain of organ music that greeted her was the wrinkled old, pipe-filled, felt-hatted face guarding the stage entrance. He was absorbed in his paper, and she let the minutes go by till her dry throat could be trusted with what she wanted to say.

"Excuse me. I'm trying to find somebody to ask if they need any singers here in this show. I wonder if you could help me, please?"

The pipe came out and the hat went back.

"Who told you to come in here?" he said. "Don't you know that everything b'way a' talent in a the-ayter is brung in here b'an agent?" He doesn't sound New York at all, she thought, he sounds Middle West. He looked at her under his wiry eyebrows for a moment, let the front legs of his chair drop with a thud, and selected a page from his paper which he tore out and handed to her. "They's a dozen or more agents listed there."

Fedalia took the torn page. "Thank you very much," she said, turning to the door. He said, "Wait a minute. Wanta go in back and watch the show?"

"Thank you, sir. Ever so much. That'd be just fine."

"Just stand over there under them steps."

The doorman was showing her where to stand, when an iron stairway clattered overhead. Fedalia looked up. A little dancing girl tripped down the stairs and passed right in front of her, ending up clear over where the edge of the stage began. The stairs kept clattering as more and more shining girls followed along, lining up in order, chattering the whole time, louder or softer, depending upon how close they happened to be to the actual stage. They had white stiff stand-out skirts which kept the line from closing up. A man in overalls hurried to the front of the line and backed along it, trying to slap each girl on the back of her bare legs as he passed. "Close up, ya chubby little jail-bait, close up!"

The girls paid no attention except to edge up closer to each other. A girl in front of Fedalia said, "Having fun, Mr. Feely-feely?" He slapped her again and said, "Not much, with those high doughnuts they hang on you ballet babes. Close up." The next girl in the line said, "You'd be in there pitchin' even if we wore cactus pants." The man came back. "Whatsamatta with you? You don't like my bathtub gin any more?"

"Oh sure, Bandanna. I was only kiddin'." The lights went up as a big brassy orchestra sound suddenly took the place of the organ music and the line of beautiful girls danced out onto the stage.

Fedalia went back to the stage door. The doorman said, "Aren't you goin' to stay for the show?" Fedalia said, "Well —thank you very much. . . . I think—thank you—ever so much." She went through the door into the alley and back onto Broadway.

The man with the tall fur hat was still calling out the same things. It wasn't even noon yet, but people were so crowded on the sidewalk you had to go with the stream, downtown if you were close to the building, and uptown if you were next to the curb.

The conversations were all through the nose, Fedalia thought, and it made everybody sound like they were saying just about the same things and mostly about themselves.

"Yeh, but lemme tell what I told 'em——"

"Five singles, he gives me, and wait'll I tell yez what I sez to 'm——"

"An are-inge drink at Nedick's, he offers me! Listen to what I told the fly-by-night."

Maybe the dancing girls and the overall man put on a little extra just to shock that greenhorn girl they saw standing there. Well, they had certainly succeeded.

The upstream flow had already taken her to the middle of the next block where a stained-glass church-looking front of a building was inhaling and exhaling a great many people, hot and tired-looking. A place to eat. And she was hungry.

Fedalia followed the people in and did as they did, putting nickels in different slots, till she had a cheese sandwich and a glass of milk. Then she sat down at a table with quite a few others. She was getting used to the nasal talk.

"I woodn-a done that a-tall. I'd-a said——"

"Now, you take me, f'rinstance——"

"Who do ya think you are? I sez. And then I told him. . . ."

CHAPTER FIFTEEN

On her way back to New Jersey the crowds on the
subway completely distracted Fedalia. Otherwise the
train's screaming plunge through the tunnel would have had
her struggling back up to the street at the next stop. She
didn't understand how the train's sliding doors could slice
off one load after another from the big, squirming chunk of
people on the platform without tearing off some of its thousand heads and arms and legs.

After four or five stops she saw that the doors had soft,
flappy rubber edges. Also, they jumped back of their own
accord every time they pushed into anyone. It was reassuring
to her that somebody had carefully worked out a way to pro-
tect the arms and legs of all those people.

It was reassuring, too, to think that everyone had so much
confidence in the brilliant mechanical-minded stranger who
thought up those doors, whoever he might be.

She began to get used to the hot, sweaty smells and the lurching and the flashing, and then she even got used to the idea of someday getting used to this scrambling, shrieking, crashing hullabaloo.

Her arms were beginning to cramp from having to keep them stuck out over the people all squeezed and jammed into her. She tried to bring her tired bones down to a little more comfortable level. It seemed as though the one who was behind her could give way just a little instead of forcing up so tightly against her. She turned her head over her left shoulder, which brought her eyes right into a man's face, wet and grinning. As he looked at her his grin slipped down at one corner and he dropped his eyes as he said something like "Excuse me" and moved back.

The ferry again. It was cold, even inside, out of the fall wind. The sky was full of racing clouds. Now that she was on the last lap of her day's journey Fedalia began to feel excited about her first day in New York. Papa would have been glad that she had gotten along so well with so many strangers and new things. And I'm not afraid. At least I'm not afraid for very long.

The West Guage bus went two blocks past her stop on Armory Street before Fedalia could get out. She found the driver wouldn't wait for you unless you kept calling, "Out, please. Out, please."

It was nice to walk along a street with trees again after the day in New York. She was anxious to tell Uncle George about finding Broadway so easily and about going into the theater, eating for five nickels at the Automat, visiting the agencies she'd found in the doorman's *Variety* till she was afraid of getting caught in the rain, then coming home on the subway, the ferry, and the bus without making a single mistake.

She had more agencies to visit tomorrow and a place to look up, a café, the one agency man had said, where a girl was needed. When she had told the man she was a singer, he had laughed and said, "All the better."

"Lemme see 'em," the agency man had said the very first thing. She'd said, "I don't know what you mean." He didn't answer her and appeared to be thinking of other things. Then he said, "Never mind," and wrote out the café's address on a slip of paper for her.

Just as she thought she might be on the wrong street, Fedalia turned the corner into the long empty block with her uncle's vine-covered house back in the trees. It had taken her much longer to get home than to go to New York in the morning. Thunder was rumbling, along with some lightning. Thunder and lightning are two things I thought I knew all about, Fedalia thought as she turned into the narrow overrun walk leading back to Uncle George's small house. Back home, though, it usually didn't thunder so late in the fall— a flash lit up the cloud banks—or lightning, either. Fedalia stood on the porch steps for a second to see if the thunderclap would follow. It did, but it didn't cover up the sound of a cat crying with fright. Fedalia called, "Uncle George!" and rattled the hooked screen door. There was no more sound. Fedalia shook the door again just as the dim hall light was turned on and Uncle George came out onto the porch.

"Uncle George, wasn't that Raggy just now? I heard such an awful screech——"

"Safely back, Fedalia? Why—yes, Raggy. I was out of the room for a moment and the poor thing got the cord twisted in some way."

"The cord, Uncle George?"

"I keep her—that is—tied for safety's sake."

Fedalia followed her uncle into the dim living room with its vined windows. She sat down in the rocker. Uncle George reached across her to snap the switch under a heavy leaded-glass lamp on the table behind her.

As the light came on she saw a letter lying under the lamp. It was addressed to her.

"Isn't that letter for me, Uncle George?" she said without touching it.

"The letter? Oh—yes. It came in the afternoon post, as an absolute matter of fact." He handed her the letter. "The return indicates a Mrs. Sutlough, as you see. The postmark is that of your home."

"Thank you, Uncle George. It must be about Papa. I think I'll read it later, if that's all right."

"By all manner of means."

The rain had started and was hitting gently on the vines. Uncle George was looking at her, but not at her face.

"I wish Aunt Bernette were here, Uncle George," she said. Her lips stuck together when she talked. Her uncle was looking at her mouth when he spoke.

"Your Aunt Bernette has been dead for three months, Fedalia," he said.

Fedalia sat still in the rocker. She said, "Uncle George, you have a peculiar way of looking at people which is very frightening. I know you don't mean it that way——"

"Why, by no manner of means. I——" Uncle George's clipped, methodical manner was suddenly gone.

Fedalia hurried on: "I know you don't mean it, the way you jump out with things. Like saying 'Aunt Bernette's dead.' It's very hard to realize Aunt Bernette is dead. Why didn't you write that to Papa?"

"Well—now——"

She said, "I just thought I'd better say how I felt because I'm sure you wouldn't want to go on frightening me."

Uncle George sat down on the small settee over by the porch window, but he got up quickly and went to the hall double doors. Fedalia said, "Maybe you'd like to talk about Aunt Bernette, Uncle George?" Uncle George turned. "If she was so sick," Fedalia went on, "you should feel her passing away was a blessing."

Fedalia would have been very relieved if Uncle George had responded to her mention of "passing away" with the familiar "I know" on an inhale, like everybody did back in Fort Madison when you spoke of death, but he didn't answer her at all. "If Aunt Bernette passed away three months ago," she said, "that was even before you answered Papa's letter last summer." Uncle George still didn't answer.

After a few moments, when he did speak, thinning up his lips over his graying teeth, there was no apology or regret in his tone.

"I don't wish to talk just now about your late aunt Bernette." He exploded the final *t*'s just slightly: your *late aunt Bernette*, biting them off with three slight flourishes of his head in alternating directions.

Fedalia stood up. Uncle George was hand-rubbing polite again, saying with regained assurance and his small forward bow, "Your trip East would have been postponed indefinitely, perhaps, would it not? If your father had known about Bernette, I mean? And wouldn't that have been very unfair? Not to say—ah—needless? My action was only in the interest of an intriguing young niece of mine whom I had only met through your father's very inadequate—as I have since learned —description. You know? Now, in view of the storm, good sense would favor your having a hot cup of tea with me and then retiring—here." He walked over to her and put his thick, short forearm on her shoulders, touching her neck with a small cold hand.

"Thank you, Uncle George"—she couldn't help moving away—"but I'm just uneasy taking up your room and I'd feel better over at the rooming house. The rain won't bother me at all." She went quickly past him into the hall.

"As you wish. Did my sister try to question you last night?"

"I must go, Uncle George. No, your sister didn't want to talk at all. She wasn't very polite to me, but the room is just fine for now, and I'll probably get used to your sister when I know her."

Uncle George came over close. "That isn't advisable at all," he said.

Fedalia felt behind her for the screen-door hook. "Anyway, I'll be going to New York early tomorrow," she said. "I may get a job in a café. On Eleventh Street. I'll let you know how it turns out." She unhooked the screen behind her and backed down the steps and kept backing down the walk.

"Good night, then, Uncle George."

He started across the porch. "I'll walk over there with you." He reached the porch steps.

"Please don't bother. I'll just run on." She started running. "It's almost dry under the trees," she called back. "Good night."

She kept running the rest of the long empty block, slowing to a walk at the corner. Her heels made an echo on the empty street, a loud echo that would easily carry back to Uncle George's front porch. She started running again because it seemed impolite, after running, to slow down still within earshot. She didn't exactly know why.

As she turned from Miss Broder's front walk to go around the side of the house, she was certain from the quickly extinguished light on the second floor that she was being watched. She also realized that from that elevation Miss Broder could keep a very good eye on Uncle George's house in the next block. Somehow this thought comforted rather than frightened her.

The metal-pipe stairway was nearly overgrown with vines,

now so wet with rain that Fedalia's clothes were dripping when she finally got to her room. The curtain didn't work over the window, so she undressed in the dark. Singing to herself ought to help the nervousness at being alone in this dark strange place.

Rose of the Ri-o Grande—Rose of the Bor-der Land—One word then hand in hand—We'll leave the preacher's side room—Hap-py lit-tle bride and bridegroom . . . The reason Charlie Landry always came into her mind at that place in the song was because she had run into him right at that place going to the paper with Uncle George's letter that day. Charlie could have come to the depot, though. Maybe there was some reason the boys would know about when they wrote. Maybe he just didn't want to come, or forgot.

Anyway, it seemed like he kept crowding into her mind as if he wanted to tell her, looking at her just as plainly as if he were here; shy grin, freckles sprinkled over his nose, and one black curl always straggling over his forehead . . . She got into her kimono, turned on the light, and sat down in the small rocker. Now she would let all the thoughts slow down. No need for any more putting off. At last she was alone with the end of her first New York day and Mrs. Sutlough's letter.

CHAPTER SIXTEEN

The clock on the Times Building pointed to eleven-thirty as Fedalia stepped out of the subway next morning. Miss Broder hadn't been too nice at the rooming house. The first thing she said as she saw Fedalia and her bags coming down the metal pipe was, "I hope you don't expect no rebate. You paid for a week, and if you walk out ahead a' time, that's your hard luck."

That was the first thing she said, and also the last thing. Fedalia remembered saying good-by without getting any response.

The subway guard had told her to get off one stop before Times Square at Penn Station to check the grip and the telescope in the depot, but the train started before she could get off. Now that she was here in Times Square it didn't seem good sense to go back. The café appointment was at two. She could pick out another agency on her *Variety* list to visit before dinner, or lunch, as they call it, and maybe leave her bags there. Then she could do something about finding a room during the lunch hour.

Her list mentioned a Hunter's Talent Bureau on Forty-fourth Street and Sixth Avenue—"Avenya," they said here—which would be one long cross-town block to Sixth, then two little blocks uptown to Forty-fourth. She could walk it easily.

Writing the note to leave under Uncle George's door had taken longer than she thought. But his not being home left her no choice. She hoped he would understand that her decision to try living in New York was because of her being able to save time and bus and ferry fares. If he thought it was also because she was afraid of him, all right, she was. She must get that café job today, though, or she'd have to spend for her room out of the emergency fund.

She stopped along Sixth Avenue to stretch her fingers and change the telescope over to the other hand. Immediately a man in a tan suit came up to her and picked up the bags. "This stuff is too heavy for a doll like you. Where to, sweet hot?" Fedalia looked at the man's grin with astonishment.

"I'm going another block up Sixth," she said. "You don't want to carry my bags, do you really?"

"Well, now look, sweet hot . . ."

"Thank you, but I'm very anxious to get one more block up this street where I have a business call to make." She reached for the handles.

"Now wait a minute, doll. I've got a proposition that's all play and no work for a young doll like you. Just being nice to guys here and there." He picked up the bags.

Fedalia said, "I could start off by being nice to you. I certainly didn't mean to be rude." They started along the street. "It's real nice of you to offer me a job, but Papa always said, 'A division of interest is weakening,' and my job has got to be singing."

"Yeah? Well, I got sump'n else in mind that'll make you sing better. Whadaya got in this square bag here, bricks?"

Fedalia laughed. "I should say not. I can't tell you how nice it is for you to carry those things. Back in Fort Madison they kept telling me New York people aren't friendly. And here my second day in town a gentleman picks up my bags in this busy street and helps me with them just like I'd known him all my life. I guess Hunter's Agency is in this block."

"What's the number you want?"

"It just said Forty-fourth Street and Sixth Avenue."

"Must be over there. Now look, sister." He dropped the bags and stretched out his fingers. Long, pale, thin fingers.

"Funny you should call me that. Papa did. And the boys too. My two brothers, Ernie and Jess. They're younger than I am and still back in Fort Madison." She looked into his face and put out her hand. "Thank you ever so much. I don't even know your name. I'm Fedalia Parker."

He looked at her and shifted his eyes away, putting the back of his hand against his mouth. "That's all right. Well— good luck on your business apperntment, sweet hot. Bye-bye."

"Good-by, then, and thank you ever so much."

The man straightened his flowered tie, took off his gray felt hat, and immediately put it back on. Then he walked out into the street.

Fedalia looked at her list and concluded the agency was on the other corner. She waited for the light to change.

CHAPTER SEVENTEEN

Hunter's Talent Bureau was on the fourth floor and required lights in the daytime, which had been the case with all the New York offices Fedalia had visited. The boy at the desk seemed to be only old enough for an office boy.

"I'd like to see the gentleman in charge," she said. The boy took his time about answering while he chewed the skin around his thumbnail.

"In chahge a' what, babe?"

"In charge of hiring singers, I guess you'd say," Fedalia said.

"You sing too?" He tipped his head over like he was trying to look all around her.

"All I do is sing," Fedalia said.

"Wanna bet?" Someone came in behind her. "Hello, Mr. Goinell," the boy said.

Fedalia first noticed manicured nails and soft fingers holding a cream-colored cigarette holder. Then she saw two small black eyes looking at her from a very tanned face on a pudgy body dressed in a gray flannel coat and dark trousers.

"Where's Hunter?" he said to the office boy, although he addressed the remark right at Fedalia.

"He's upstays in the rehoisal hall, Mr. Goinell. He's expeckin' yeh. Yeh want I should get'm feh yeh?"

"I'll wait awhile."

The boy went back to chewing his thumb. Mr. Gurnell walked across the small lobby to a short leather couch, stopping in front of the telescope and the grip.

"Oh, I'm sorry!" Fedalia hurriedly ran over to slide her bags out of the way.

"Perfectly okay, child, perfectly okay. You waiting to see Hunter?"

"Yes, sir, I guess so."

"Well, sit down. I'm Tom Gurnell."

"How do you do? I'm Fedalia Parker. I can't wait too long, though. I've got to find some place to leave these bags and get a room and eat lunch and be down at the Full-Moon Café on Eleventh Street all by two o'clock."

"Well. Looks like you need some help, girlie-girl. You know Hunter?"

"No, sir. I just found the Hunter Talent Bureau in Variety. I'm a singer, Mr. Gurnell, and I need to get a job right today." Mr. Gurnell was looking at Fedalia. He didn't pay any attention to the small dark girl with enormous high heels who had come in and walked up to the desk. Her voice was flat and cutting.

"Hey, hey, Fuzz. What's around?" she said.

"Nuthin' great, Shorty."

"I mean anything at all, Fuzz. I'm stranded from a turkey.

Send me to any kinda call—burleekew, anything. They must be some calls around."

"Full-Moon Café down in the Village. Two o'clock. 'T'sall I know."

"In your hat, Buster. Full-Moon is right. That's what you gotta show down at that dive. It's a fish-bowl trick down at the Full-Moon, and this ain't the day I'm givin' away any sight auditions of me. See y'around." She clicked sharply across the floor and out.

Fedalia looked quickly back at Mr. Gurnell, guiltily realizing that she had obviously and frankly listened to everything the girl had said.

Mr. Gurnell said, "I thought you said you were a singer."

"I am, Mr. Gurnell. They told me at the other agency that they wanted a singer at that Full-Moon Café."

"Well, I guess they wouldn't mind your singing. Nobody could hear you, though. You'd be lying nicely curled up naked in a big fish bowl, girlie-girl, visible to the select patrons in a cute little bar they keep hidden from the cops down there."

Fedalia felt sick in her stomach. She was grateful for the arm that fell around her shoulders.

"Too bad, child, but that's show business. Expect something classy and it turns out crummy. Come over to my office tomorrow—or better yet"—he looked at his wrist watch— "come along with me right now and let's see what we can work out for you over a spot of lunch. You know, you have a soloistic personality for my dough. Where did you get those two Mediterraneans you use for eyes?"

He pulled her to her feet.

"Tell Hunter I'll be back, Fuzz."

"Yeh, Mr. Goinell."

"I'll pick up these bags later. Come on, girlie-girl."

He kept his arm around her all the way down the elevator, stood behind her when they reached street level, then steered her out the door by her arms.

"There you are, child, and I guess the quickest way to get to Eugenie's is to walk."

"What's Eugenie's?"

"A 'speak' over on Forty-eighth Street. God's teeth—you've never been to Eugenie's?"

"I don't think so. If you mean it's a speakeasy, I've never been to one."

"Well, in five minutes from now you won't be able to say that, sober or not."

They went through the janitor's door under the stairs of a Forty-ninth Street brownstone front into a place that looked like a living room converted into a small restaurant. The waiter bowed to her and spoke to Mr. Gurnell, disappeared while they were sitting down, and returned a few moments later with two cups and saucers containing a little water in each cup, only Fedalia discovered it wasn't water, it was fire.

She coughed and Mr. Gurnell seemed very surprised and pleased as he said, "You mean you've really never been to a speakeasy before—haven't even had a drink before?"

"Mr. Gurnell——"

"Call me Tom, child." The waiter put down two plates full of cold meat and cheese, peppers and olives.

"It's funny how you call me 'child,' Mr. Gurnell. You're not that much older than I am."

"That's why you should call me Tom. I call you 'child' because you're so sweet and adorable." He took another cup from the waiter and drank it all in a gulp.

"Well, about the singing, Mr. Gurnell——"

"What else can I call you besides 'child'?"

"My name is Fedalia."

"God's teeth! I can't call you Fedalia. How's if I call you Fiddle, sweet thing?"

"All right . . . I guess . . . Fiddle? That's not very pretty."

"A fiddle gives out pretty music when it's played by somebody who knows how to play it, and I draw a nasty bow, Fiddle, my child."

Fedalia said, "I've got to get a job right today, Mr. Gurnell."

"Well, let's get away from all these mundane people and discuss the sitcheashun thoroughly. I guess if it's Mundane at Eugenie's here, it's probably Thursdane up in my place. At least I'd like to have you spend from now till Thursdane making fiddle music up at my place. Fiddle, my child, what reaction do I hear?"

"I ought to be getting along as soon as we finish, Mr. Gurnell."

"That's exackatickely what I mean, Fiddle. You ought to be getting along and me right along with you, and my name is not Mister Gurnell, it's Tom. Say, maybe I'll start calling you Jerry, then we'd be hot stuff together, Tom and Jerry."

"I don't have any room even. I thought sure I'd get that café job and then hunt up a place to stay."

"Look, girlie-girl. You are going at this thing entirely backwards. These small-time agents are flesh boys. If you gotta go to an agency, go to one of the big high-class ones. Or better yet. You want to sing. Well, all right. Before you make the rounds of all the leg-and-prat-fall bookers, go where the tonsils come first, get me? A broadcasting station, for instance. Waiter, get me the check. Where's the phone?"

The waiter pointed to a sagging phone booth in the hallway, and Mr. Gurnell got up.

"Be back in 'arf a mo'. I know everybody over at the ABCA network and I'll fix you up with an audition *just—like—*

that." He accented the words with three pinches under her chin and left the table.

I wonder if he's drunk, Fedalia thought. He's the strangest-talking man I ever met. She could see him talking in the booth. He hung up in a few moments and came out, making a circle sign in the air with his thumb and forefinger, which he pushed in her direction several times on the way back to the table.

"ABCA at four-fifteen this afternoon, child. Regular Friday auditions. If you go at three you can run your songs over with the piano player. It's only two now. Got time for another drink and in the meanwhile I'll think about a place where you can stay."

Then abruptly he started talking Southern.

"Yassuh, yassuh, Magnol-i-a, mah little Dixie belle. How does that sound to you-all, honey chile?"

"Well, thank you. I——"

He dropped the Southern talk. "Look, child. I may be casting a new show next week. It's a musical that would pay you maybe sixty-two fifty a week; would you like that, child?"

"Mr. Gurnell! What would I do for all that money?"

"Sing. A solo spot, of course."

"A solo spot? Why, you've never even heard me sing a note. How can you make me an offer like that?"

"I happen to be the producer of the show, and you get a solo spot when I give the word, and I give the word when you give the word——"

"I don't know if I understand what you mean exactly, Mr. Gurnell."

"Look, you sweet little adorable thing, you. I live on Central Park West in a 'bachelor' that's got a view of the park, also a very discreet landlord. You can move into the plans for the new show, and my life, the same day. The very same day. How about it, Fiddle?"

100

"Mr. Gurnell . . . I . . ."

"Don't look at me like that. God's teeth. Call me at this number after you audition. Now, I'm off. Tallyho, my girl, stout fellow, shoulder to the wheel, chin up!" He picked up the check. "Got a small deal to put over in the marts of trade yet today. Waiter! Here you are, my man. This young lady will leisurely finish her scoff and leave when she desires. I'm buzzing off now, Fiddle. Thank you veddy much, rawther, quite and cheerio."

CHAPTER EIGHTEEN

"A. B. Wixberry's office, Miss Jern speaking." Mr. Wixberry got up and walked quietly to the door, hating his own artificial deliberation. In his mind he slammed the door as violently as possible. Actually, he just barely pushed it to with exasperated gentleness. A. B. Wixberry, A. B. Wixberry, A. B. Wixberry. On these audition Fridays he was strictly a mental case, he was free to admit, so susceptible to irritation that any form of repetitious sound became a Chinese water torture, even the sound of his own name.

He sat down again and crossed his legs, then immediately uncrossed them. A young executive must be razor-pressed at all times, he reminded himself sarcastically. Only old V.P.s could sit around in baggy pants, spilling cigar ashes all over their vests.

He fiddled with his black pencil mustache irritably, he patted the four white starched points in the breast pocket of his blue suit irritably, he rested his right forefinger under his pointed nose and smelled of it irritably, then he lit a cigarette and blew out a lungful at the wick of his silver lighter. That was supposed to be bad for a lighter, he'd heard. He wished he could extinguish as easily the futile ambitions of the would-be singers, actors, and actresses flutteringly awaiting audition down the hall. If he were running the Amalgamated Broadcasting Company of America, the first thing he would do would be to abolish audition day, public relations be hanged.

Audition day—Black Friday. In his entire career as ABCA's program director he had yet to hear any one of those bleating, emoting, stage-struck exhibitionists show enough talent to qualify for amateur night in Carnarsie. Why not, for God's sake, staff your station with experienced people? Not amateurs, protégés, squirming, incompetent, doll-faced, desperate tremble-chins.

Helen Jern came in from the outer office to turn on the big speaker in the corner. Mr. Wixberry said, "Well, Helen, so far we've had two 'My Heros,' a 'Bell Song,' a Nazimova impersonation, and a couple of 'Mother Machrees.' This has got to be a baritone."

The loud-speaker interrupted: ". . . singing 'The Toreador Song' from *Carmen*."

"I don't know about this one at all," Miss Jern said in a puzzled voice. "I can't understand this baritone not being on my list." Mr. Wixberry folded his arms quietly and nodded his head, pushing his lips out in exaggerated thoughtfulness. He listened for a while with a certain fascination. "Isn't it marvelous the way he stuffs that moth-eaten march down your throat?"

Then he viciously killed off his cigarette in the ash tray at his elbow. Miss Jern snapped off the speaker without having to be told.

"Any more?" he said without looking up.

"Just one, Mr. Wixberry." Miss Jern spoke quickly. "Tom Gurnell, who has sent up people before——"

"Who?"

"Tom Gurnell. He's a producer and he's requested you to hear a friend of his, a girl singer, a Miss Parker, Mr. Wixberry, and she's due at four-fifteen."

Mr. Wixberry prowled around among his papers and drawers for another cigarette. The search ultimately took him to his overcoat hanging in the outer office. He arrived there one split second before a perspiring second-string left-guard type burst in, flinging the door from him as if it were the back of his hand. *The Toreador*. Mr. Wixberry winced at the wilted crimson carnation in the young man's buttonhole that clashed badly with his fiery red hair. The boy looked around wildly.

"Where's Mr. Wixberry, the program director? I just sang 'The Toreador Song' for him!"

Mr. Wixberry calmly said, "Is that so? I know you won't believe this, young man, but I've heard that march before. On the Friday auditions, too." He took as much time as he possibly could locating his spare pack of cigarettes in his overcoat pocket. When he could trust himself to go on he said, "I'm Wixberry," and took out a cigarette, holding it unlit as he leaned back on the edge of Miss Jern's desk. He looked at the young man. "My friend, that was as fulsome a rendition of 'The Toreador Song' as I have ever heard. You sang it with no evidence of talent or ability whatever. You sang the high notes sharp. You sang the low notes flat. You phrased everything backwards, and I couldn't tell whether you were singing in French or Italian. Will—ah——" He put the cigarette to his lips and moistened the end of it. "Will you answer me one question? Why do you insist on doing something you have no qualifications for?"

The young man started to answer, shaking his head, then seemed to change his mind.

"I'm sorry," A. B. Wixberry said as he went back into his office, shutting the door behind him. He snapped a flame out of his lighter on the third try, then looked at his watch. "How can I possibly listen to that Parker girl today?" he said to his secretary. "It's already four, and I have to be on Long Island by five-thirty."

"Couldn't you be a little late, Mr. Wixberry? After all, if it's just a routine cocktail party——"

"Miss Jern, if there's anybody around here who needs the small diversion of a 'routine cocktail party' any more than I do, I'd like to know who he is, and since when do you grade and classify my social activities? And for God's sake, you know the girl can't possibly be any good—they never are—and answer the phone!"

Miss Jern went out to her desk.

"A. B. Wixberry's office. Miss Jern speaking." Mr. Wixberry jumped up, but Miss Jern had already kicked the door shut. In a moment she came back in. "Miss Parker is due in ten minutes. Shall I take some dictation?"

"No, Helen." Mr. Wixberry crossed his legs. "I will sit here comfortably in this chair and do nothing for those ten minutes. Then I will listen to your Miss Parker. Then I will go to my routine cocktail party, providing, of course, that plan meets with your approval." He took a remote pleasure in Miss Jern's blush as she left his office and closed the door.

"Fedalia Parker, please. One song will be ample."

"But I have sort of a routine of three."

"We're already fifteen minutes behind schedule. I'd suggest the popular ballad. Emil, here's Miss Parker's music. She wants it a tone up."

"Always the same thing!" the pianist growled. "That puts

us up in B major with a mess a' sharps. You know, for a coupla bucks you dames could get your stuff copied over in the right key. Ever think of that? Oh-oh, there's the red light. Let's go!"

The studio abruptly started to spin around. The arpeggio Fedalia got for her introduction bore no resemblance to anything she'd ever heard before. Desperately, but without success, she tried to see a funny side to it all. Then she had to open her mouth and start, somehow. Before she could recover any sense of reality it was all over and she was gathering up her music.

It couldn't possibly be over so soon after all the waiting and planning, but it was. It was all over. She knew she hadn't done well at all. Maybe if she could find the big man himself, that Mr. Wixberry, she could tell him about the strange arpeggio and the transposition and that she hadn't planned to start with a ballad at all.

She hurried out into the lobby, past the reception desk, over to the left-hand corridor to the first office up front. A. B. Wixberry, Program Director, it said on the door.

"Mr. Wixberry just left," the lady in the outer office said. "Maybe you can catch him at the elevator."

Catch him at the elevator, I've just got to. He'll understand I was nervous. That's him! That's got to be him.

If he'd only wait . . . "Did you hear my audition, please, sir, Mr. Wixberry?"

He didn't turn around. Maybe he hadn't heard her question. Then he answered her over his shoulder. "If you're Miss Something Parker, my audition report says No in capital letters."

The elevator door slammed shut.

"Not to get personal or anything, dear, but can that possibly be your own hair? And clear across the lobby I could tell that there should be a law prohibiting the size of such deep, gorgeous blue——"

Fedalia turned around almost into the arms of a curly-headed young man in a gray-blue suit. It was too late to do anything about the tear that squeezed out on her cheek.

"Well—say—I'm sorry," he said. "You didn't let old iron-heart Wixberry really get to you, now did you, dear?"

"It's just that——" She stopped. Children always begin explaining their tears with "It's just that . . ." She was a grown girl, on her own in New York. . . . She started again. "I've come all the way from Fort Madison, Iowa, where ever since I was thirteen years old I practiced and worked for a New York audition. And it does seem as though Mr. Wixberry could have said more to me than just 'no' without even turning around. . . ."

"Why, that big bag of hot air! Come on!" He pushed her into a waiting elevator and pressed something into the operator's hand. "Advance Merry Christmas, Mac," he said. "Let's go down without any stops, hey, lad? Emergency."

"Yes, sir." The operator slid the door shut, and when they got down to the ground floor Mr. Wixberry was standing in the lobby complaining to the elevator starter about something.

The young man followed Fedalia out of the elevator, tipped his hat, and said, "Excuse me a moment." Then he placed his hand on Mr. Wixberry's shoulder and edged him around. Fedalia got a three-quarter view of a youthful gray felt hat, a thin black eyebrow, a medium-long and sharp nose, a thin black mustache beneath it, and an open inquiring mouth with white teeth. His chin was bluish and trimmed with the edge of a white scarf.

The young man hit him hard, right on that medium-long nose. Mr. Wixberry staggered back and fell to the floor without a word, as Fedalia incredulously watched the white scarf begin to absorb droppings of red. The curly-headed stranger took her elbow and said loudly, "My name is Spartan Coliss. Am I going your way?"

As they started away Fedalia glanced back at Mr. Wixberry, who was still on the tile floor—taking no apparent interest in their departure—or in anything else.

CHAPTER NINETEEN

Adelbert Wixberry had grown up in Fargo, North Dakota. He had always been skinny and thin, and when he was seven they made him a pair of black velvet pants.

Those black velvet pants were partly to blame for his being so stubborn that Christmas. He hated everything about them, beginning with the little peephole in the front that would never stay closed, and he was anything but grateful for being trusted with the last climactic piece to recite just before Mr. Kleek came out as Santa Claus to break down the garden wall and give a "brick" to each child.

Adelbert made a frank attempt to close his little peephole. Then he stepped up to the edge of the platform, but he didn't open his mouth. His mother whispered from the front pew, "Go on, Adelbert! 'On a starry night . . .' Go on—go on!" It was some time before he finally did conclude the Christmas exercises with these words: "I said I wouldn't say it and I won't."

He was unhappy for other reasons besides the velvet pants. He hated his name, for one thing. Every time he moved up a grade his mother would always tell the new teacher, "Accent on the second syllable, if you please." All his life he had wanted a nickname at school and nobody ever gave him one. He guessed the kids just didn't like him well enough because maybe he was a coward. He'd suspected that about himself down in his heart for a long time. He didn't think he was scared of being hit, though. He had never had a fight— didn't even know how you were supposed to stand. He was more embarrassed about looking awkward and flailing away clumsily and maybe falling down than worrying about being hurt. And how do you know who is supposed to hit first? And do you put your thumb inside your fist or outside, and should you hit for the person's nose or mouth or what?

For another thing, there was a force of conformity down inside of him that made him feel different from the other kids, something he couldn't do anything about. All his life he had accepted law and order, the theater manager's authority over the picture show, Mr. Kleek's authority over the Sunday school, Miss Brown's authority over the public library, Miss Pabalot's authority in the classroom. Like last Halloween, when they were out in the neighborhood switching people's garbage cans around and holding lighted pumpkin faces up to the windows to scare people with. The big North Side kid suggested getting the grocery wagon out of the alley back of the store and pulling it down to the footbridge and dumping her over into the creek. Adelbert went along while the kids got the wagon, but he kept begging them not to really dump it in the creek, till they called him a sissy-pants and made him go home.

He couldn't explain how he felt about just breaking up people's property like that, and not because he was scared of being arrested or anything either.

110

The big kids talked about the rubber hose the principal had in his office and bragged about how many times they had been licked with it. Adelbert's imagination had never taken him into an actual scene of being hit with The Rubber Hose. He didn't even have a mental picture of what a rubber hose was and whether it would hurt or not. He was just horror-struck at the idea of violating authority to the extent of having to be sent to the principal's office. . . .

It was nearing the end of the term and the class had been noisy and restless all week. By the time Friday came around Miss Pabalot was in a bad mood. When somebody happened to be whispering pretty loud during spelling she got up and came straight down the aisle to Adelbert's desk. "Young man, go to the principal's office and tell him you couldn't stop whispering." A few unreal moments passed and he found himself out in the empty hall with all the other kids in the rooms where they belonged. He'd never even spoken to the principal in his whole life. He slowly went down the creaking stairs and out into the schoolyard that was only deserted like this when the teacher sent you on an errand or when you came panting across it trying to beat the tardy bell.

That whistling noise his green corduroy knickerbockers made didn't give him the usual goose-pimples now. He didn't hear anything or see anything till he got clear home and found himself out in the back yard trying to realize what had happened.

His father got home just after the noon whistle had brought the world back into a normal focus, but Adelbert didn't know what to tell nor how to tell it. He ate some of his dinner and automatically started back up the street for school. Standing in line for the last bell, the kids whispered questions about "the old man" and "the rubber hose." Adelbert just swallowed and tried unsuccessfully to grin. The teacher met him at the door with her hand out for the admit.

"The admit?" he said.

"Yes, young man, the admit. When you're sent to the principal's office he gives you an admit to return to your class. Go get it, please."

The only thing Adelbert could remember clearly about the next fifteen minutes was the sarcastic way the principal said, "Well, why did you go home?" His only answer was, "I guess I don't know why." If only the principal had got out the rubber hose or yelled at him or slapped him instead of just reaching out for his pad in cold contempt.

He looked up over his glasses before starting to write. "Adelbert, eh? I better shorten that name up for you." He filled out the admit and handed it over.

Adelbert couldn't help the tears that were smarting his eyes by the time he got back upstairs again. He hurriedly wiped them on his sleeve as he stood outside the classroom, turning the paper over and over again in his hand. It was written in pencil, and there was his big red eraser right in his pocket which might easily have smeared over the writing, but he knew he'd never try it. He had to go through that door with his new nickname written just like it was on the small slip—nothing could change that.

He went into the room in front of all the kids and up to the desk, his chin on his chest, and handed the teacher the admit, made out to "Dolly" Wixberry.

Maybe Miss Pabalot would keep it to herself. But Adelbert knew he didn't believe that, even as he thought it. Miss Pabalot so often seemed to enjoy being mean just to be mean. Still, maybe she wouldn't read the admit out loud . . . just maybe . . .

He went into the room and up to the desk, his eyes on the floor. Miss Pabalot put out her hand. Adelbert gave her the admit, raising his eyes just for the length of one blink, but still long enough to see his "just maybe" die in the tight smile that was forming around his teacher's lips.

Her heavy dress rustled; the ruler smacked quickly and sharply on the desk top, quieting the whispers and the giggles; her rasping inhale preceded the familiar mirthless chuckle, then the loud words.

" 'Dolly' Wixberry? Well, that's a lot easier to remember than 'Adelbert,' I must say. Dolly, you may take your seat."

Adelbert hurried to his desk as the shrieking laughter of his classmates filled the room.

"Dolleeeee . . ." Adelbert was out in back a few weeks later practicing annie-ay-over. He stopped dead in his tracks, his jackknife falling clumsily out of his hand. "Dolleeeee . . ." It was his father calling him from the front porch. His own father . . .

As soon as Adelbert Wixberry realized he was sitting on the floor in the ABCA lobby he jumped to his feet. *Crazy madman exhibitionist.* He glanced at his watch and saw with dismay that it was nearly four-thirty. He wiped his face on his already bloody scarf and hurried out into the street— stopping at the haberdasher's two doors up. He was in the midst of picking out a new white scarf when an ambulance arrived noisily in front of the building. Then a police car appeared.

Curious and briefly concerned, the passers-by were gathering halfway up the street as Mr. Wixberry and the clerk joined the crowd. At the outer edge of the sidewalk was the crushed body of a young man whose fiery red hair clashed badly with his crimson carnation and the small pool of blood it rested in. The Toreador.

CHAPTER TWENTY

A passing ambulance contributing its siren to the normal Times Square noises made conversation impractical until Fedalia and her curly-headed companion had walked several blocks up Broadway.

Fedalia swallowed and said, "That was real—gallant." The young man looked full into her face, blankly. Then he bent in the middle and started elevating and lowering the top half of his body like a bellows. "Gallant, yet—— Oh no!"

Fedalia had no idea what Mr. Coliss was laughing at so hard.

"What a first-act curtain," he gasped. "Everything but a silk hat and an illegitimate chee-ild." He went off into another howl, pumping at the waist again. When he finally stopped laughing he said abruptly, "This Wixberry is the worst kind of a man I ever heard of. I should-a picked him up and smacked him again. You know I've been coming to

ABCA for six months, at least twice a week, trying to get in to show that joker a coupla songs? And he always turns me over to some musical director named Henry Helb, as though it was the first time he'd ever talked to me. Well, he'll remember me now, maybe, next time we meet. Where are we going?"

"I thought you were going to the subway. I have to pick up my bags over on Sixth Avenue and find a room. Unless I want to call Mr. Gurnell first."

Mr. Coliss said, "Now here, this is the remark of a highly irrational young woman. Who's Mr. Gurnell? The only thing I can think of to assuage your shattered nerves would be a cup of tea at yonder chop suey joint." He guided her firmly off the curb out into Broadway. Fedalia wondered why everybody in this town insisted on risking their lives when they had the red and green lights to go by at the corner.

They reached the other side safely and in a few moments were running up the one flight of stairs to the chop suey place as though they had a train to catch.

The restaurant was empty, big, and rambling with heavy black furniture and long gold, purple, and red lanterns. They sat down in a booth by a big window that looked out on Broadway.

"Pork and egg roll," Mr. Coliss said to the waiter who had appeared with a huge pot of tea and two little cups as soon as they sat down. "Now, Isolde, what's your name? I'm Spartan Coliss, as I believe I mentioned, and besides hitting program directors in the beak I write lyrics."

"How do you do, Mr. Coliss. My name is Fedalia Parker."

"Fedalia?"

"You rhyme it with Australia."

"Maybe I will. It's an interesting lyric idea. And you want to act on the radio. Why?"

"Well, not exactly. I started going to agencies to get on

the stage, but Mr. Gurnell said the broadcasting studios would be better."

"Oh, he did? Who's he?"

"A producer I met at Hunter's Talent Bureau. That's where I left my bags. He was going to help me get a room later."

"Oh-oh . . . You mean you just got off the train from—— Where'd you say?"

"Fort Madison. That's in Iowa, but I came to New Jersey to live with my uncle Broder, I mean Uncle George. But it takes such a long time to go back and forth from New Jersey that I decided today I'd better come to live in New York. But I have to get a job real soon to pay expenses. Then I want to get a teacher——"

The waiter interrupted with the cold pork and a dish of small things that looked to Fedalia like little raw cinnamon rolls before baking, only yellow and fluffy.

"I'm not real hungry, Mr. Coliss," Fedalia said, but Mr. Coliss didn't pay any attention and pushed some of each kind off onto her plate.

"You will be when you try those, Gorgeous. Call me Spart, will you, dear? You dunk the pork in the mustard and then in this red stuff. Sugar in your tea?"

"Yes, please." He took the lid off the teapot and put several spoonfuls of sugar right in the pot, shook it around a little and poured their cups full.

"A room for this gorgeous girl." He squinted his eyes and looked off some far place over her shoulder. "This big-eyed nymph. Big eyes are always thought of as oche chorrrnia. I never saw blue eyes the size of yours. Never even thought there was such a thing. Or are they brown?"

"Well . . ."

"You're too good to be true, Gorgeous. Describe you in a book or put you on a stage, you and all this gold and blue . . . Ah. Nobody'd believe it."

116

"I think it's very nice of you——"

"A room for this girl . . . You won't believe it, but I'm thinking about taking you home to my sister Florabelle. And this move, mark you, lass, is very out of character for me, I assure you." He burst out with another of his wild laughs. " 'Florabelle, since reading about Tom Swift at Annapolis, I decided to bring home this beautiful golden-haired, chameleon-eyed maid, who rhymes with Australia, in the hope, the eager hope, that you will allow me to consider inviting her to the Senior Prom!' "

Fedalia laughed agreeably while Spart gulped down his tea. "No kidding, Gorgeous. I think I'll take you over to my sister's neighborhood at that. She lives on top of a flower store she's been trying to run. Over on the East Side. This is in a block that sort of watches old Avenue A's crummy atmosphere blend into the beginnings of the new swanky East Side —sitting there on the fringe, as it were. The real estate boys will get around to it any day now, but in the meantime there's a walk-up or two with some nice clean one-room working-girl kitchenettes here and there. Lots of broadcasting slaves over there."

"That sounds like just the thing if I would be able to afford it."

"Fifteen, sixteen smackers a week, furnished."

"Oh . . . Well, if I got some kind of a job right away. Spart, maybe your sister needs somebody in her flower store."

"She certainly does. Customers. I thought you wanted a job at a radio station."

"Well, just until I have a little better luck than I had today, and not enough to cause a division of interest. You know, I worked at Mr. Quimby's greenhouse in Fort Madison when I was small, and I get along wonderfully with growing things. I'd like to help your sister, maybe mornings, even if she didn't pay me anything. Maybe I could get a room for

117

ten dollars. That would give me—well—for five weeks I could get along without having to earn anything, and by that time——"

"Hmmmm, I see. In other words, you don't have what you'd call a large kitty."

"I beg your pardon?"

"Can you tell me why we are sitting here writing plots in this joint? Let's get down to facts, dear. Maybe Florabelle needs a helper-outer. Maybe there's a quiet southern exposure with concealed plumbing waiting for you right around the corner at your own price. Let's, for the Lord's sake, find out. Let's get your bags and sca-ram over to the east side. Waiter?"

"I'll have to call Mr. Gurnell," Fedalia said.

"Why?"

"Because I told him I would." Fedalia got up and went over to a phone booth she could see near the cashier's counter and called the number she had written down. "Mr. Gurnell, please," she said to the lady that answered. "Fedalia Parker."

Mr. Gurnell was still English. "What jolly well ho, Fiddle. Shall we get your jolly old reticules and 'op it over to my diggings?"

"Mr. Gurnell, thank you ever so much, but could I call you tomorrow and tell you about my audition and maybe sing for you over at your office? You're a lot too important to worry about my bags and my room and all like that, Mr. Gurnell. So I'll——"

"Now, Fiddle, my child—wot's all this 'ere?"

"I think I've got a room lined up and I don't want to bother you, but if you'd like to hear me sing a little later on——"

"Okay. You can reach me at this number afternoons." His voice was suddenly flat, but at least she could understand him.

"Thanks ever so much, Mr. Gurnell. I'll call. Good-by."

There was only just time to say hello to Florabelle Coliss in the flower store because, contrary to Spart's pessimistic remark about no customers, there were five people in there all trying to get waited on. Spart's sister impressed Fedalia as a familiar type of big Iowa farm woman just now sniffling with an irritating cold. Miss Coliss's startled glance at her brother when they walked in with the bags made it plain that she thought he was crazy.

"See you later, Sis," Spart called from the door. "Take some sulphur and molasses or something."

Fedalia said, "Pleased to've met you." They crossed the street and continued three doors farther along to a dull-looking building of dark red brick.

"Sixth floor rear," said the lady who answered the bell. "Kitchenette. Toilet and tub down the hall. Fourteen dollars in advance. No lease."

Spart said, "She'll take it. Can we go up?" The lady reached behind her and brought out a key. Fedalia thought about the fund pinned inside her underwear.

"I'll pay the fourteen dollars on my way out to supper—dinner," she said. The lady looked significantly at Spart.

"I'm just going to take the bags up," he said. By the time they reached the top they were both panting.

The room was dark and small, but it appeared to be clean from the quick glance Fedalia nervously gave it. Spart put down the bags and said, "Come over to the store later. Bang on the door if the shades are down. This isn't the Waldorf-Astoria, is it? But it's homey in a disturbing sort of way. Well, then, wear it in good health, dear. Bye-bye." He blew her a kiss and walked out.

Fedalia dropped onto the couch-cot. New York! And she had a room of her own and some new friends, even if she had been such a failure at the audition. Mr. Wixberry was certainly unfair to judge her voice in such a way. She got to thinking about his big broadcasting studio and that she had really sung over there this very afternoon! Pretty good to get in there at all on her first day of New York job hunting, and go through an ordeal like that.

She'd get another letter right off to the boys before she did another living thing. She took her tablet out of the telescope and wrote very briefly about moving from Uncle George's. Then she told about ABCA and her earth-shaking experience:

. . . and the young man hit Mr. Wixberry smack on the nose! Can you believe it? I thought for a moment I was watching a flicker at the Bijou. Nobody said anything at all and we just walked away. And now, of course, I haven't any job or any contact even at ABCA, but I found out that the young man, whose name is Spartan Coliss, has a sister who runs a flower store, and I've got a room for fourteen dollars a week right in the same block! He's tall with black curly hair like Charlie Landry's and wears the longest points on his shirt collar you've ever seen. He smiles most of the time and has a dimple in his chin, like Mr. Purdy. I saw his sister, and the next time I pass the store I'll talk to her about my helping with the flowers until I get my singing job. Of course I was a little disappointed with the way the audition turned out, but a radio station isn't the only road to the opera house, by any means. Something will turn up, I'm sure, and everything happens for the best, anyway. I don't think you boys could remember, but Mama used to always say, "Success is the string that holds together a necklace of priceless failures." Priceless! That's what my experience was today. Look how much I learned: Be ready with one number in case they haven't time for three. Insist on a rehearsal. They'll respect you for it, and I'll have the music in the right key next time even if I have to copy it myself.

I'm sure you must have written by this time. I'll send Uncle George my address and answer your letter as soon as he sends it to me. I was wondering if you happened to see Charlie Landry on the way back from the depot. Please don't worry about me, and I won't worry about you as soon as I hear from you about things. What are you doing about your meals? Maybe it would be better for you to board out somewhere for a good supper every night. Please thank Mrs. Sutlough for writing me about the funeral. I'd have come home on the next train, but you know Papa would not want me to do that. So I'll just keep on the best way I can. If Charlie Landry won his race I guess I can win mine. Remember back that spring when he beat out Moose Felt and Shink Burns and all those great big guys?

Well, please write and don't worry about me and I won't worry about you.

Love
Sister

CHAPTER TWENTY-ONE

Fedalia sealed up the letter, thinking it would be fun to hunt up a New York City mailbox after she put her clothes away. It didn't take her long to transfer the things from her bags to the drawers of the large old dresser —the most important piece of furniture in the room. Then she washed her hands and face in the kitchenette sink, and had just finished tidying her hair when there was a brief knock at the door. Before she could answer, Spart walked in. He dropped an armful of packages on the table.

"There's tomorrow's breakfast, Gorgeous. And by the way, my sister Florabelle is expecting you at the store in the morning. Do you know anything about cut flowers and wiring corsages?"

Fedalia said, "Well——"

"Neither do I—you'll just have to ad-lib till you get the hang of it."

He walked over to the room's only chair and sat down. Fedalia unwrapped coffee, cream, sugar, and pastry. "Spart! You shouldn't have brought me all this."

"We'll argue about that later, Gorgeous. Why don't you sit down and rest that elegant little frame of yours?"

Fedalia sat down on the couch-cot. Spart slid down in his chair.

"What'll we talk about?"

Fedalia said, "I'd like to hear some more about the show business."

"Not *the* show business, dear, just show business."

"Oh. Do you know Al Jolson, Spart?"

"Sure I know Mr. Jolson, dear, and Ben Bernie and Eddie Cantor. Though I'm not sure they know me—yet. There's five or six hundred of us belonging to the Friars Club, and we're not all stars, by any means."

"It must be wonderful, Spartan. Do they have other poets there besides you?"

"Lyric writers, Fedalia, not poets. My sitting over here on this side of the room, by the way, is merely a disciplinary measure. You and your cornflower, wide-eyed innocent, girl-woman . . ." Spart closed his eyes, clenched his fists, and shook them a few times over his head. Then he swallowed, opened his eyes, and quietly continued.

"Sure, there's lots of other lyric writers—like Larry Hart, the fellow I told you about with the inside rhymes, and Gus Edwards, and the daddy of 'em all, Gus Kahn."

"I like Ben Bernie's music on the phonograph. Especially the railroad song. That's my favorite; you know it, Spart?"

"Yeah." Spart moved over onto the couch-cot with Fedalia.

"It's a cute song, but the lyric in the bridge stinks with a crash."

"The bridge?"

"The middle, the middle where it says, 'I'm the sun, the sun that's cryin' for to shine.' "

"What's the matter with that?"

"Everything, Gorgeous. This is a big cliché, you understand? The first thing you got to understand about writing anything is get away from clichés, see?"

"I'm not sure I understand what you're talking about, Spart. How would you improve on 'I'm the sun that's crying for to shine' in the railroad song?"

"Fedalia, this is a cinch. Let's see here. In the song this line means I'm a fellow that longs to get to the big city and strut his stuff, right? How about, 'I'm a mermaid sighin' for the Rhine'? Or, 'I'm a stale beer lyin' in the stein'? Or, 'I'm a grape that's dyin' to be wine' or, 'dyin' on the vine' or—— I've got it! 'I'm an old shoe cryin' for a shine'!"

"Spart, you're wonderful! How can you do it so fast like that?"

"Lyrics are torture to write. I mean good ones."

"But you do it so easy."

"Not good ones, Gorgeous. I've been working on one lyric now for seven months and getting no-place. And this is a funny thing—you get a few rhymes, not only at the end of the lines, but inside—smart rhymes like Larry Hart, and right away you're hypnotized momentarily into believing you got it. You breathe freely for the first time in days, like an emancipated soul, like you've just been left a million dollars, like you've just been kissed by Gloria Swanson, like you're Webster just putting the last period in his dictionary, like you're a knitting woman hooking the last stitch in a rug for Madison Square Garden—and then comes morning and with your first waking effort you say over your wonderful lines and what do you think?"

"What?"

"They stink with a crash."

"Maybe you just get in the habit of changing your lyrics all the time, picking at them and 'improving' them."

"Oh no. When a lyric is done it pops up inside you just like toast in an automatic toaster and nobody has to tell you it's ready. There she sits."

"Let me see the lyric you're worrying over now, Spart."

"It's called 'Every Day,' and it is the ungrateful, sneering beast of a serpent's tooth of a thankless, blood-sucking title that's making all the trouble—Every Day."

"That's a *beautiful* title, Spartan. What's the matter with it?"

"I don't know—it just won't let the lyric happen. Look at this:

> "Ev'ry day love songs are written
>   by fools who are smitten with love,
> And so I try to find a few simple phrases
>   to impress you as I sing your praises.
> Ev'ry night dreams make me clever
> And still I can never get through,
> Can't get beyond 'I love you, darling, I do'
> Every day!"

"Spart, that's a wonderful poem!"

"This may be a wonderful poem, but it's a lousy lyric."

"Why?"

"I don't know why! I told you, it just isn't right. Here's another quart of blood:

> "Ev'ry day you're like the sunrise,
>   So near yet so far, far away—
> And like a distant star that shines through the
>   twilight
> You're the high light that I wait all day for—
> Then each night, you're like an angel

My dreams find the way to your charms
Please leave the dreams and come to stay in
    my arms
Every day."

"Spartan Coliss, I never heard any better words in my
whole born days! You're too critical."

"There's no such thing as being too critical. Look,
honey—— What's the matter? I'm not going to bite you. I'm
just momentarily holding your hand. . . . You got to be
critical or you end up with nothing. You can't get anybody's
attention away from himself without a real trick. I mean the
public. They won't tumble unless you trip them with a trick.
This goes for books, paintings, music, and lyrics, as I said
before."

"How do you mean a trick, Spart?"

"A trick is something unusual and intriguing that nobody
thought of before, and the only way to find this trick is to
not kid yourself like the amateur lyric writer and the greenhorn composer I knew once. They completed their brain
child and tried it through in loud excited voices for the
first time. When they finished, the composer grabbed his
collaborator by the hand with a triumphant gleam in his eye
like Balboa discovering the Pacific, and yelled, 'It fits!' "

Fedalia had to laugh, even though she was getting nervous
and damp in her palms with Spart squeezing over closer to
her by the moment.

"Honey, the thing is not to beat your brains out searching
for the good part. The job is to keep throwing out the bad,
unoriginal stuff. Got to learn to recognize the bad stuff and
throw it out. If you keep doing that long enough you're going
to end up with a good hunk and maybe a trick."

"Spart, if you don't mind, I——"

"Hold still. Ever see Beethoven's sketchbooks? This was

a genius purely and simply because he recognized what was no good. Go over to the big library with the lions in front next time you're on Fifth Avenue. For a study in torture, take a look at some of Beethoven's sketches. He starts a couple of bars of perfectly respectable music, but he knows it's not right so he immediately writes the whole thing over with one phrase upside down. I say immediately, because it looks like it happens this way on the paper. Actually, he has hammered his insides with his own fists for hours and days and weeks getting this alternative for what he knew was no good. But he still isn't satisfied. Under his second try is another, right side up this time, but with grace notes. Then another try with sixteenth notes instead of eighths, and on and on till God only knows how many sleepless hours later the simple magnificent opening theme in the slow movement of his Fifth Symphony sits there on the paper just right and he knows there's nothing bad left in it, and therefore it must be good, and this has stayed good for one hundred and fifty years, and if I'm such lousy company that I can't sit next to you on the sofa with my arm around you, I better run along."

"No, Spartan, please. . . . I'll put some coffee on. . . . I——"

"Good night, and thanks a lot. I'll stop at the shop and tell my sister to expect you in the morning."

CHAPTER TWENTY-TWO

It was barely eight the next morning when Fedalia opened the front door of Florabelle's Flowers. She found Miss Coliss all the way in the back.

"Morning, Miss Coliss. How're you feeling?"

"Now how should I be feeling? No more deliveries from downtown till I pay up. No decent cuts—nothing to sell for the week-end trade but a bowlful of brake fern and some what-the-deuce lemon leaf. Got a big funeral coming up tomorrow, and I couldn't even stuff one plaque unless I cut up my long underwear. Haven't got a three-inch pick in the place, so how do I handle maidenhair? Which doesn't matter anyway because we're fresh outa maidenhair too. If Otto Kahn walked through that door offering fifty bucks for a corsage, I'd have to make it outa huckleberry and curlicue, and you ask me how am I feeling?"

Fedalia murmured, "I'm sorry, Miss Coliss," which she

didn't think Miss Coliss heard because she didn't say it very loud. She said it again.

"Don't call me 'Miss Coliss.' Am I your old-maid aunt?"

"I'm sorry, Florabelle." She said it good and loud this time, but of course now it referred to calling Florabelle "Miss Coliss" and not to her trouble. Florabelle deserved to know what she really meant, feeling troubled and all. "I'm sorry about the store, I meant—the bills downtown . . ." Florabelle didn't answer, but that was all right. Fedalia knew she'd heard the remark, at least, and it's better than nothing to know somebody is sorry when you're in trouble. "And when I asked how were you feeling I was thinking about your cold." Florabelle ignored that too. Then she dropped a large wad of wet newspaper onto the floor and, putting her hands squarely on her hips, she looked directly at Fedalia.

"So my lady-killer brother picks up a stage-struck blonde and dumps her in my lap," she said, "with the simple explanation that she likes flowers."

"Well, I just happened to mention that I used to help out in Mr. Quimby's greenhouse back in Fort Madison and he——"

"Back where?"

"In Fort Madison. That's in Iowa."

"I thought only Indians and cows came from Iowa. I need a helper on my pay roll like I need a burr up my nose, not that I'm not short-handed, but I'll have to pay you off in carnations."

"Oh, I didn't expect any pay, Florabelle—not at first. But until I get a radio job—singing for money someplace—I——"

"Well, at least you can take a few meals with me upstairs. That'll save some wear and tear on your budget. Say, you are a blonde. And how could you have such fer-cryin'-out-loud huge blue eyes or whatever they are and still have room for

129

that pink, innocent kisser? I'm beginning to understand why Spart lost his nerve and brought you over here instead of—— Didn't he even mention Atlantic City?"

"I don't think——"

"Or the Hudson River night boat?"

The door opened and closed in the front. Florabelle peered out past the icebox as a young priest entered the store. "Gotta keep the busted stuff myself, Father," she called out. "It's all I got to sell today." Fedalia saw the priest smile and wave his hand as he went out. "Maybe I should have asked that priest to pray for some credit for me," Florabelle said, wiping her nose on a handful of asparagus fern. "Looks like the time for some desperate move like that."

"Why don't you do it yourself?" Fedalia said.

"What do you mean, pray? I certainly wasn't serious about asking for help from the Cloth."

"It might be better to do it yourself, anyway. Who else knows exactly what you think you want?"

"Look, what's your name again?"

"Fedalia Parker."

"Look, Fedalia Parker." Florabelle reached up on a hook behind her and tossed over a purple smock. "All the praying I know is Spart's big mealtime joke, 'Thanks for the butter, thanks for the meat, thanks for the soup,' and so on. Plus, of course, 'Our Father, which art in heaven.' That I can rattle off like anybody else, just in case I get caught at a funeral or Christmas exercises or something. But I don't think that would take care of this situation."

"I don't either, Florabelle. You ought to make it up. I used to say 'Now-I-lay-me' every night till I—well, I wanted something special once and when I tried to put it in words— you know—to ask for this certain thing, I found the certain thing I was going to ask for seemed a lot less important than I'd thought. At least not important enough to discuss like

130

that—you know—with God. It was like I'd got His attention and He very kindly laid aside His business and said, 'Well, now, what can I do for you?' and then when I had the floor I was ashamed to grab for this or that thing for myself and just ended up being glad for being healthy and saying, 'Bless Mama and Papa and Ernie and Jess, Amen.'"

"Well, for your private information, squirt, if at any time I ever feel that I've got the ear of the Almighty, I'll have no hesitancy about cold-turkeying Him for some cash on the line so I can keep this store open."

"Maybe you will, Florabelle. But if you think about it sometime—— What's that expression of Spart's? Ad-lib! Try to ad-lib a prayer for your special trouble and see what happens."

"Okay, okay. Did my brother give out enough trade secrets last night to let me risk turning you loose with a trayful of gardenias and a green salad?"

"I guess not, Florabelle. We got to talking, and the time——"

"All about his lyrics, of course. However, he doesn't know much about flowers, anyway, or he'd know how tough this racket is and help out with a few bucks like he's always promising and always forgetting. Just use your wits and keep your eyes open and be your own teacher. You'll see more and remember more."

"I'll sure try hard. And I really didn't expect you to pay me anything. I just love to be around flowers someway."

"We'll see, and there's the morning's first customer. Oh-oh. It's Helen Jern. Be polite to her, Fedalia, while I get my smock on."

Fedalia walked up to a very trim little lady who reminded her of the privet hedge around Farmer Garvey's front yard.

"Good morning. Would you like to buy some flowers?"

"Don't tell me Florabelle has a clerk? Where have I seen you before?" The lady put her thumb up to her teeth.

131

"I don't know, ma'am."

"Didn't you come frantically into my office yesterday looking for the boss? You're a singer! You're—Bordello Plunkett, or something."

"Fedalia Parker. How you could remember me out of so many——"

"Not so many that look like you look. I'm Helen Jern."

Florabelle interrupted, "And the scars you would see on her back if she dropped her shift are made from the black-snake whip of old Massa Wixberry. She's his amanuensis."

"You are!"

"His secretary."

"Well! How do you do, Miss Jern."

"Whatever he said to you in the hall was below the belt, I know that. Please believe me, we're not all that way over at Amalgamated."

"Oh, I know that, Miss Jern. Can I help you with some flowers?"

"From singing to flowers, just like that?"

"Oh, it's only for the time being."

"I'll take that small bunch of whatever-they-are for my desk. Somebody's got to buy something from this Coliss woman. Well, I'm glad to find you, and don't be discouraged. Singing is a tough business to be in. I won't forget you if anything turns up. Sometimes I feel like ABCA's conscience. Hey! I gotta get on my horse. G'by, girls."

"Say, Helen," Florabelle said. "Your boss might not make it this morning. Spart stopped by on his way home last night with the news that he poked Wixie in the nose yesterday down in the lobby of the ABCA building."

"What! Your brother did? Why?"

"He just got carried away with Blondie here. He resented Wixie's opinion of her audition and—you know—swung on him. Wonder somebody doesn't do it every day. Run on, gal.

I'll give you the play-by-play later. You're late already, and if Adelpate does come in, you know he'll be in a mood."

"Well, I'll—be—darned. Did he know it was Spart who hit him?"

"Spart says Wixie never seems to know him, even when he gets a look at him, which this time he apparently didn't."

"I've spoken to Mr. Wixberry half a dozen times about Spart Coliss and his lyrics. Wonder what he'd think if he realized he was fractured by a poet last night. Well, this will be an interesting morning in the talking-bottle factory. Florabelle, I'm really late, see you tonight."

"Watch yourself, Helen."

Helen Jern expertly flipped her cigarette into the street as she waved. Florabelle gave Fedalia a handful of rags and a hand mop to use on the floor of the north show window and went on back to the stock room.

Fedalia thought about how Mama used to call everybody back home who smoked a "cigarette feend," like Mr. Huntley who managed the Bijou. He couldn't have smoked half as much as Miss Jern, probably. . . .

As Mr. Wixberry walked into his office Miss Jern was adjusting a small bunch of flowers on his desk. He started to take one for his lapel as she said, "Good morning. Did you hear about the boy falling off our roof yesterday afternoon after you left?"

Mr. Wixberry replaced the flower in the vase—straightened up.

"Yes, I did, Helen. I——"

"There it is in the paper. No, over on the second section, inside. His mother says there was no possibility that he jumped. They've always had height-phobia in their family, she said, and the boy must have just got dizzy and fell over.

That's all it says. Wonder what he was doing in our building. Here's the mail, Mr. Wixberry."

He took the handful of letters and walked into his office. He closed the door and slumped down into the big chair behind the desk. Was suicide in this town so commonplace that the identity of the singer wasn't already run down by everybody in the studio? By what curious circumstance had the tabloids overlooked the chance to headline ASPIRING RADIO SINGER PLAYS TRAGIC SUICIDE ROLE? Maybe the boy hadn't said anything to his mother about the audition. Maybe he'd just slipped in without any appointment. Maybe his name wasn't even on file. Maybe a lot of things. No need to keep it a secret, though; yet nothing whatever was to be gained by telling anyone till they asked. The boy had sung "The Toreador Song" and had pried out his opinion just before "falling" off the roof. . . . An *unimportant detail*, he thought, *but not unimportant to me.*

CHAPTER TWENTY-THREE

Fedalia hadn't seen Spart for several days. "He disappears like this every so often," Florabelle said. "Usually women or work. This time I feel it must be work, with you stashed away over here where he could get at you. He'll show any day now."

But two Sundays went by and no Spart. Fedalia was getting used to Florabelle's talk, and she was happy to be some help in the shop, even though she only worked mornings. Afternoons were spent waiting in agency offices, but she had yet to get another chance at any kind of audition. Helen stopped in often for a few flowers and a visit. Because she had said there might be a chorus job at ABCA, Fedalia spent her evenings running over scales as best she could without a piano, to keep her voice ready. She sang as quietly as possible and not later than ten. Most of her meals were taken with Florabelle in the small flat over the store, noons and evenings.

The boys had written her several times from home. They had written before to Uncle George's address, they said. Fedalia wondered why Uncle George hadn't forwarded the letter. She had sent him two cards with her new address on each, telling him about giving an audition at ABCA and also about Miss Jern encouraging her with some hope of a chorus job.

She was thinking about Miss Jern one Monday morning just as Helen entered the store with a rush.

"Fee, I'm in a jam and you've got to help me out and I know you won't even consider it."

"Of course I will, Helen."

"Oh no, you won't. But I've got no choice but to ask you anyhow. My boss, of whom I know you must be extraordinarily fond, told me three days ago to get reservations at the St. Regis for tonight—for four people—himself and Grantham Turner and me—I usually get rung in on these agency-men excursions."

"Well . . ."

"And a girl for Turner. That's the part I forgot."

"Now, *Helen!*"

"Honey, his agency is picking up quite a lot of radio billing these days."

"I don't like agencies."

"He runs an advertising agency, not a talent agency. Please, Fedalia . . . I'm already late for the office, and there's no use trying to get anybody down at the studio."

"There must be a lot of girls down at ABCA you could get."

"Not with a cocktail dress in their handbags to change into."

"But, Helen, I haven't got a cocktail dress."

"Oh yes, you have, dearie—for tonight, anyway. I've got my number-two glamour outfit in this grip, and the number-one creation is hanging in my flat waiting for you. Forget you ever heard of A. B. Wixberry, just for tonight. Can't you please, Fee? He's a different guy away from that office, and I guarantee he won't know you from a hatrack, or even your name. . . . Singers—particularly female ones—are just wraiths that pass in and out of his loud-speaker. Honest. I'm late, Fedalia darling. See you at the office at six, and be there now, Fee, please. Here's the key to my flat. Try on slips or shoes or anything you want, but be there!"

Helen Jern raced out the door and down the street. Fedalia said helplessly, "Florabelle . . ."

"Now, honey." Florabelle put down an azalea pot and took Fedalia by her shoulders. "I'm not suggesting that you turn the other cheek or anything, but I do think you should do Helen the favor. You can just sort of grin and bear it for an evening, can't you?"

"Oh, Florabelle . . ."

"Besides, you'll be with the other guy, who will no doubt bend your ear the whole evening, and it will be easy to ignore Mr. Wixberry."

"Do you really think I should go?"

"Thatta girl! Don't worry, kid. If you lose control and strangle Wixberry I'll hide you in the cellar for a few short years until it blows over."

Customers started coming in and Fedalia did her best to keep the hours from ticking away, but no matter how her spirit pulled back, five-thirty arrived and there she was in the middle of Helen's number-one cocktail dress, looking at herself in the long narrow door mirror which alone lifted these small ladylike two rooms and a bath up to a level of luxury far beyond any actual setting she'd even dreamed of.

A mirror in a door! Maybe she'd have one to dress in front of when she started singing professionally. She'd have to have several evening dresses like this. The career she and

Papa and the boys had talked of and worked for so hard began to fill up her imagination again, as it had before she left Fort Madison.

If Helen Jern got her a chorus job, she would find a teacher and start her singing lessons again. Think of her knowing an important radio woman like Helen Jern, and standing here in a rustling silk dress, being able to see all of herself at the same time in her successful friend's mirror!

Helen phoned while she was dressing to say she'd pick her up in a taxi in ten minutes. Fedalia was waiting as the cab drew up.

"Helen, what if he recognizes me?"

"He's not going to recognize you in a million years. Get in. And he doesn't make sarcastic remarks except to people on audition days who can't wait for the report."

"You've never given an audition or you'd understand how frantic you get."

"Fee, you can tell me about anything except how frantic you feel at auditions. I'm the frantic expert, remember? Now, sit back."

In a short time the taxi pulled up in front of a high East Side apartment house fitted out with a glittering glass canopy and a doorman.

"Helen, this is a big mistake. I feel it in my bones. Tell him I'm sick and couldn't make it. It won't be a lie. I never felt any sicker in my whole born days."

Helen pushed the taxi door open.

"Up and at 'em, ya big sissy."

The driver handed Helen her change and the doorman led them under the canopy to the wide double doors of the apartment building. Regretting every step, Fedalia followed Helen into the elevator and up to the threshold of 19B. A small white card in a dignified slot read *Adelbert B. Wixberry.*

"We might as well push the button," Fedalia said, just to see if she could still talk.

Mr. Wixberry answered the door. "Good for you," he said to Helen. "You're the on-timest girl."

"Mr. Wixberry, this is Miss Parker."

"How do you do, Miss Parker. It was so nice of you to come."

"How do you do, sir."

"Want to get some ice, Helen?" He took Fedalia's arm to lead her into the most beautiful room she had ever been in, with thick soft carpet and a grand piano. And a fireplace. He stepped over to a heavy dark red drape and pulled it back.

"Helen tells me you're a newcomer to our town. Take a look at this. Doesn't New York look beautiful from here? That's the East River over there." She looked out at the view. "But I guess it's all a matter of perspective, and I don't mean to belittle perspective either. Quite the contrary." Fedalia stepped closer to the window looking down at the lights nineteen stories below. "In a way," he went on, "the proper focus on things is largely what distinguishes mediocrity from greatness, isn't it?" Fedalia looked without answering.

After a moment he said: "A genius, for instance, always seemed to me to be an artist who could add the last crowning strokes to his canvas without having to step back. Anybody can see the beauty of New York from here. Down there it takes a great deal more perception, don't you think?"

Fedalia said, "After the wonderful faraway view from here, close up it would be like looking at something through a microscope, I guess. My brother Jess made me look at a lightning bug one time under his microscope. He won it selling perfume soap lockets from the Sunday paper."

"I got a magic lantern that way once myself, only I sold bluing. Did the lightning bug wiggle?"

"It wiggled and looked so hairy and ugly, I never would

139

look through that microscope again. But I love lightning bugs when they stay little and graceful."

"Well, Miss Parker . . . New York can look pretty ugly and frightening up close, I guess, but don't let it worry you. Any time you need reassuring, come up to my office and I'll show you New York from forty stories up. That kind of perspective really gives the Old Lady dignity and charm." His eyes were on hers for a moment.

Some hearty new baritone overtones behind them indicated that Mr. Turner must have arrived.

Mr. Grantham Turner could have been English, the way he talked, but it seemed his natural way. He called Mr. Wixberry "Bart, old boy," and when Fedalia told him she was from Iowa, he said, "Had no idea the Middle West produced such teddibly attractive gyels." He was huge and looked at Fedalia under heavy dark eyebrows; in fact, he had a suggestion of heavy dark hair every place but on his head, which was almost bare. Mr. Wixberry served drinks from a shiny little table of glass and silver. Fedalia said, "No, thank you," and he didn't comment or appear surprised in any way.

On the way to dinner Mr. Turner didn't put up the back of the taxi's little folding seat and sat facing her. Then he apologized for his big knees during the entire trip.

The St. Regis dining room was pink and gray and softly lighted. An orchestra was playing.

Fedalia hadn't thought about the possibility of being asked to dance at all when Mr. Wixberry asked her. She said, "I don't think I'd better, if you'll excuse me."

"Of course." Again he made no comment, nor did he act surprised.

After the first part of the dinner had been served Mr. Turner and Helen got up to dance. Mr. Wixberry offered her a cigarette. She shook her head.

He smiled. "Don't drink, don't dance, don't smoke. Well, what'll we do now?"

"You must be from the Middle West, Mr. Wixberry," Fedalia said. "You don't say broad a's like so many in New York."

"I certainly am from the Middle West, the wild and woolly West, from the New Yorker's point of view. I come from the Dakotas. Injun country."

"Papa used to say that a real Winnebago will chase a little old Dakota Injun till hell won't have it again. He wasn't really cussin', Mr. Wixberry. That's just one of Farmer Garvey's old sayings back home."

"My grandfather played the guitar."

"So did mine. He used to sing a wonderful song about 'Keemo kimo—derro art—me hi—me ho—me humdrum pennywinkle tit tat pitty pat blue-eyed pussy cat sing song kitty, can't you ky-me-oh.'"

"And what in the world do those words mean, Miss Parker?"

"My name is Fedalia. You rhyme it with Australia."

"Ah—Fedalia—mine is Adelbert. Accent on the second syllable."

"Adelbert? What do they call you for short?"

"I—ah—just Adelbert, unless you're English like Granny Turner. He loves to call me Bart. Never really had a nickname. I like Fedalia. Seems to me it ought to mean 'faith.' I seem to remember *fidelis* means 'faithful' in Latin. In fact, there is a Sousa March dedicated to the Marine Corps called 'Semper Fidelis'—Always Faithful."

"There is?"

"You'd know it if you heard it." He hummed a familiar melody, then broke off to say, "Haven't you a couple of sisters named Spes and Caritas? Meaning——"

"Hope and Charity. I took high school Latin too, Mr. Wixberry."

141

"Adelbert."

"Adelbert. No, I haven't any sisters, but I have two brothers named Ernest and Jess. Jess is just out of high school and Ernie is nearly out of Horatio Alger."

"Which I don't suppose you would know anything about, Fedalia."

"Yes, I do. I read *Sink or Swim* from cover to cover. All my life I have been hoping to run into somebody in real life who says 'in course' for 'of course' like all Alger's characters do, but I haven't yet."

"I'd forgotten how that used to irritate me too. Ah— can't you tell me what that song of your grampa's meant?"

"Grandpa died before we ever found out. He did tell us, though, about the last line: 'Sing song kitty, can't you ky-me-oh' means 'Sing song kitty, can't you cry meow?' I guess the rest was sort of made up from that."

"I guess it must have been. What do you do? I mean, what kind of work are you interested in?"

"Just now I'm a florist helper-outer over at the flower shop where Miss Jern gets her flowers. Helen stops in almost every day for flowers for her desk."

"Yes, Helen's mentioned the great Florabelle. Now if you ever want to send me a message you can tie it to a carnation and give it to Miss Jern."

Fedalia smiled politely.

The music stopped and Mr. Turner brought Helen back to the table. Fedalia listened to the talk mostly about the radio business. When dessert was being served Fedalia said, "How can they burn those cherries like that right at the table?" She laughed and held her hands tightly together as the waiter poured hot, flaming cherries over the ice cream.

"I'm glad you're having such a good time, Fedalia," Mr. Wixberry said. "I don't know when I've enjoyed myself more."

"In the movies," Helen spoke up, "you only have real fun at an amusement park. I saw it again the other night. Halfway through the picture, when the time came to indicate 'carefree days,' sure enough, they showed one of those fade-in, fade-out scenes at Coney Island."

"I know," said Adelbert. "Technically known as montages. They usually splice three views together. First they show the hero and heroine coming lickety-split down the slide for life——"

"She's got her arms around his neck."

"I'm glad you noticed that, Fedalia." Mr. Wixberry stroked his thin mustache on both sides as though it had villainous handlebars on it.

Mr. Turner said, "The second scene is the one where the hero chap knocks over all the ducks in the shooting gallery while the gyel friend expresses great admiration."

"As she soulfully leans on the counter and looks up at him," Helen added.

"Correct," said Adelbert. "And the last scene shows them tired but happy on the trolley going home."

"And she has a lamp shade and a Kewpie doll under each arm."

"Wrong, Fedalia," Mr. Wixberry said. "I'm surprised at you. She's asleep on his shoulder, clutching a bunny rabbit, and he's got the lamp shade and the Kewpie doll. Makes him look ridiculous and extremely lovable."

As the music interrupted them Helen said, "Tomorrow's a workday, Mister Boss."

Mr. Wixberry said something to the waiter, who hunched his shoulders and nodded toward Mr. Turner. Mr. Wixberry shook his head. "What, again?" He looked across the table at Mr. Turner. "Granny, you're the greatest check-grabber I ever saw, or else I'm the most expert fumbler of all time." Mr. Turner jumped up, buttoning his jacket.

"Aw, chuck it, Bart, old boy. You can sweeten the maître dee, if you insist. Shall we do the floor once on the way out, Miss Parker?" Without waiting for an answer he pulled Fedalia out onto the dance floor. "Hope you don't mind a strong lead," he said. He was so lumbering and huge, Fedalia felt as though she could have just hung on and let her feet dangle.

"What's the mater-dee, Mr. Turner?" she said.

"The captain. The fellow in the dinner coat with the big smile."

"He seemed like the manager."

"That's the chap. One has to be nice to him in the hope the beggar may remember your name next time. That's why it was very generous of me to let Bart parcel out the farewell largess to him, so to speak."

"Our waiter ought to remember you all right. He didn't bring you any change."

"I didn't expect him to. A waiter earns his tip. A bad waiter can spoil your whole evening."

Fedalia said, "His helper worked hard too."

"You mean the bus boy? Oh, a good bus boy should always be not seen and not heard."

"He could spoil your evening, too, I should think."

"Well, I never thought of that. Odd, isn't it, how these bus-boy chaps might as well be transparent? Not only people don't pay any attention to them, they don't even see them, as though they weren't even there."

"That doesn't seem fair, exactly, does it?"

"Well, now that you speak of it . . ."

"I guess they're waiting for us, Mr. Turner." They had danced once around the floor to the entrance side. Mr. Turner took Fedalia's arm as they stepped into the path of a worried-looking bus boy, red and perspiring.

"I say, that is, son——" The bus boy looked around behind

him and saw only the wall. He looked back at Mr. Turner, frozen astonishment on his face, as though he still couldn't believe he was being spoken to. Mr. Turner handed him a bill. "Thanks for taking care of our table, young man," he said. The "young man" was about sixty, Fedalia noticed. He took the bill in his hands—looked down at it and then up again.

Mr. Wixberry came up to them. "Ready, Granny?"

"All ready, Bart, old boy. Sorry to hold you and Helen up. Haven't had a chance at this young lady all evening. Did you fix up the captain? I—ah—took care of the bus boy."

They were walking along through the lobby when Mr. Wixberry stopped abruptly. "The bus boy?"

"Why not?" Mr. Turner said. "He does more work than anybody else around here."

Mr. Wixberry shook his head with a smile. "Granny, you're the end. The absolute, positive end."

As the doorman closed the taxi door Mr. Wixberry leaned forward to speak to the driver. "Stop off first at the ABCA Building below Times Square," he said.

"Going to work already?" Mr. Turner said. "Come now, Bart. The vice-president's union will get after you for that, old boy."

"I only have to pick up some papers Helen forgot to remind me about."

"What papers, Mr. Wixberry?" Helen said, looking a little startled.

"Apparently I forgot to remind you to forget to tell me about them, Helen. No, seriously. I want to do a little juggling of the new program schedule tonight. Granny, how about lunch tomorrow? I'd like to talk over a little profit-and-loss, man-to-man stuff with you before you get to flirting too seriously with that certain new network that can't do you any good."

"Right you are, Bart. Shall we say the Astor at one?"

"Twelve-thirty would suit me better."

"Twelve-thirty. Right you are."

They passed quickly through the lights of Times Square. Too quickly to suit Fedalia.

"And here's my stop." Mr. Wixberry opened the door. "Come on, Fedalia, keep me company. Helen's put in enough time at this factory for one day. Now if the two of you end up in the Village eating soul candy and getting into trouble, don't say I didn't warn you." Mr. Wixberry jumped out of the cab and reached back for Fedalia. "Good night, and thanks for a nice dinner, Granny."

"Right you are. Good night, Miss Parker."

Fedalia said, "Good night, Mr. Turner, thank you ever so much. Good night, Helen."

The cab drove off, and Fedalia and Mr. Wixberry crossed the wide sidewalk over to the revolving door she remembered so well.

The ABCA lobby was empty except for a woman who was scrubbing away at its marble and tile. As they waited for the elevator Adelbert glanced down at the tile floor. The elevator door sprang open. Adelbert said, "Good evening, Andy. All the way, please."

The door slid shut as the electric floor numbers began to light up on the panel and black out. The lady at the reception desk was getting ready to leave as they stepped out of the elevator. Passing by her on their way through the lobby, Mr. Wixberry said, "Good night, Miss Macfadden."

"Nobody back there but 'Organ Reveries,' Mr. Wixberry."

"I know."

"Good night, Mr. Wixberry."

The hallway on the right side of the lobby ran all the way back, past all the glass doors of the studios and control rooms. "I'll lead on." Adelbert smiled back at her. A red exit light burned at the end of the long hall over a small iron railing that guarded a few steps leading up to Roof Fire-Exit. "It'll be a little dark and cold, and I hope not too windy," Adelbert said, putting his arm around her as he opened the door. Together they walked out onto the roof. It wasn't dark or windy at all, and strangely not as cold as it was on the street. A continuous background of sound rolled gently along like a mild new kind of distant automatic thunder, and the sky reflected back onto the roof top the glow it drew up from the street. They walked past air vent, water tower, and skylight, over to the edge of that silent superior world.

"It's beautiful, Adelbert." She felt his eyes on her, not on the view. But he must have seen New York from here many times before; it was only natural that he wanted to see her reaction. She turned around against the waist-high parapet. He seemed to want to show her the lonesomeness in his eyes.

"This probably seems to you like a routine," he said after a while.

"How do you mean?"

"I open up a conversation with a beautiful girl in my flat about my nineteenth-story view. I casually bring in how much better it is from forty stories up, like, say, down at the ABCA Building. Then I drop the subject. That's the clever part, hmmm? Then as an afterthought I bring up the office again on the way home, and in this way get the girl up to the roof, you see? And, oh yes, by the strangest coincidence we find that everybody's gone home, including even 'Organ Reveries' by this time. And here's the part nobody would believe: My office just happens to be on the top floor of this very building, and I *could* say the elevators have all stopped running."

Fedalia looked down over her shoulder, following the movement of a streetcar as it crawled up the dark of Seventh Avenue till it blended into the glow of Times Square. "You want me to think you're joking, Adelbert, but I don't think you are," she said. "I've never kissed a boy—a man. I nearly did once. I knew we both wanted to. We had for a long time. And when we almost did, it was as important as life must be to you when you're drowning. I mean it was a great important-feeling event like drowning would feel. But it was drowning up through clouds instead of down into water. I could explain it to Papa now, I think, if he were alive."

Adelbert shook his head. "You don't know about anything that isn't honest, do you?"

"I know 'a division of interest is always weakening,' and I think I understand people quite a bit because I know everybody is made up of the same things as everybody else, only in different amounts. And I don't think you ever kissed a girl for the reason Charlie Landry wanted to kiss me."

"Now *just* a minute . . ." Adelbert pulled Fedalia upright against him with one quick arm. She felt his other hand back of her head and his breath on her lips. He whispered, "I'm honest too." Then he let her go. "I'm honest, and proud, and a coward. In that order." He took a cigarette case out of his coat pocket. Fedalia watched him light his cigarette and exhale a jet of smoke.

"You couldn't be, in that order," she heard herself say.

"What has the order to do with it?"

"A coward is a coward first of all, I should think. And he couldn't be either honest or proud, could he? A coward is sure to run into times when he would be afraid to be honest."

"Or afraid not to be."

"And he certainly couldn't have any pride if he was a real coward."

"All right. A few weeks ago a young guy knocked me down in the lobby of this building and walked away. Song-writer fellow I've seen around. Why haven't I hunted him up and had it out? I don't honestly know if I'm afraid to or not."

"Being scared has nothing to do with being a coward. But you'd have to know first why he knocked you down and whether he was right or not."

"What difference would that make?"

"Not any. But you'd have to know first, I should think."

"What makes you think I don't know why he did it?"

"Do you?"

"I guess I do." Fedalia looked away, and over the city. *I was there, too,* she might say. *I've forgiven you for being so cruel, though, not because I understand it but because I know you're not cruel. Then you would say you'd make it up to me and you'd offer me a job because you're sorry. That's like Mr. Gurnell, who hasn't even heard me sing at all. Helen Jern has heard me, at least without the piano, and if she gets me the chorus job it will be on my merits.*

Adelbert was saying, "Why didn't you want to dance with me tonight?"

"I did want to."

"Why didn't you?"

"I didn't think I should."

"You danced with Turner."

"Only once around. Because he just took hold of me before I knew it."

"Don't you like to dance?"

"Papa died three weeks ago tonight."

Adelbert put his cigarette carefully down on the roof top and stepped on it. "I'm sorry, Fedalia." He picked up her hand. "Did you come all the way from Iowa to work in a flower shop?"

"No. I'll tell you about that sometime. It must be awfully late."

"Oh?" Adelbert looked at her hand. Then he raised his eyes to hers. After a moment he led her back across the roof to the door.

149

Fedalia walked on her toes over the cold bare floor to the light string hanging down in the middle of her four walls, papered a long time ago with a fading floral design, the same horrible brown, she thought, of those broken oblong cookies she used to get in the barrel at Bate's Grocery Store—"Helens" were they called? She pulled the string with a quick hard pull, and climbing back onto her squeaking, springless cot in the dark, she thought about the ropes they used to pull like that to send the money baskets back to the cashier in Gilbert's Dry-Goods Store. How she used to love to go on an errand to Gilbert's for a card of buttons or a spool of thread so she could watch the clerks put the articles and the money in one of those wire baskets. The first pull on the rope with the wooden handle lifted the basket up to the ceiling. Another pull and zing! All the way along the trolley wire, clear to the back of the store, flew the basket, rocking a little from side to side with extra speed if it came all the way from the ribbon counter up in front.

Poor faded flowers on the horrible brown wallpaper. What could she do to freshen them up a little? You can't put faded wallpaper floral designs in water. Her cot protested loudly as she turned over to the brown wall. I'll ad-lib a short prayer, she thought, and then just close my eyes and wait for the garbage-can racket to begin in the morning.

Fedalia had dreamed a lot since arriving in New York, strange dreams with tall thin people all giving vague advice after asking her to leave her name and address. But tonight she found herself dreaming one of those clear, reasonable-feeling happenings, full of detail: the sound of the door buzzer, her finger on the button for a moment to release the latch downstairs, her unwashed breakfast dishes on the tiny sink.

She opened the door to see Florabelle in her purple smock, only she had on a black artist beret. This velvet tam went well, not only with the smock, but with the black mustache and the pointed nose, because it suddenly wasn't Florabelle at all but Mr. Wixberry. He had a large bell in his hand which he rang like a scissors grinder, but it sounded like the bell over the door in Florabelle's shop.

"Any auditions today, madam? You are the lady of the house, aren't you?"

Fedalia nodded, and he went on saying, "Then-may-I-show-you-direct-from-the-home-office-for-demonstration-purposes-only-the-Wings-of-Magical-Melody-Zimmerman-Autoharp? Auditions every Friday at four o'clock."

"Are there any arpeggios on that machine?" she heard herself asking.

Mr. Wixberry looked at her sternly, shaking his head. "No arpeggios for chameleon-eyed girls who don't drink, smoke, or dance."

Papa pushed Fedalia away from the door. "Now look here, young man. Did you know my daughter behaves like a slut on the hall seat? Her mother saw her right there with Charlie Landry. Even though she was in the cemetery. But Fedalia has to have an arpeggio just the same. From the lettuce jar—because she's a genius, a real musical genius."

"I merely wanted to take her to Coney Island," Mr. Wixberry said, "for an audition at four o'clock."

"Coney Island in October?" Papa said with a sneer.

Mr. Wixberry appeared uncomfortable at this question. Papa laughed. "Well, only fifteen minutes, then. I'll wait for you on the porch."

Suddenly Mr. Wixberry had his arm around her and they were flying through the air in a small wooden green-and-red roller-coaster car. She was bumping into Mr. Turner's knees. Mr. Turner wasn't there. Only his knees. The last climactic, almost vertical dive of that roller coaster was the kind of

151

leap into space that usually concluded a dream. But she couldn't shake her way out of this one yet.

They staggered out of the wooden car and doggedly fought their way through a large crowd to the shooting gallery. Adelbert missed the ducks, almost killing the proprietor, after which Fedalia went over behind the Gila-monster tent and quietly threw up a hot dog and some crackerjack.

Adelbert gave the proprietor's wife a ten-dollar bill. She wiped her nose carefully with the bill, saying Adelbert was entitled to a lamp shade and a Kewpie doll. Then unaccountably they were in the subway. Fedalia had just noticed that the guard was Spart Coliss, when the banging noises turned into the early-morning rattle of the garbage cans down in the street which woke Fedalia up with a start.

CHAPTER TWENTY-FOUR

Mornings around ten o'clock there was invariably a lull in Florabelle's Flowers. Father Pat had come and gone, taking along a box of short-stemmed carnations and odds and ends. Fedalia had just finished telling Florabelle about her first dinner party when they saw Spart hurrying across the street. He grinned at them through the window and opened the door. "Hey, there, girls! A little respect, please." After hugging Fedalia, he tried to pick up Florabelle, purposely staggering around the store, puffing and blowing, to make him appear hopelessly bogged down by Florabelle's bulk.

"Spart, you idiot! Let go—you wanta rupture yourself?"

"Don't mind if I do. Wait till you hear about the new job I got offered me. Threllkell, Squat, and Halbeard."

Florabelle, still in her brother's bear hug, pulled away to stare at him. "What kind of jabber is that?"

"That's the name of a little two-by-four advertising agency who never had an original thought in the joint. So naturally they want me. How about this, Floozybelle?"

"I'm for pulling down the shade for half an hour and going upstairs for a cup a' coffee to hear about a few of these things."

"I've never been asked upstairs quite so out and out." Spart put the back of his hand on his hip and flopped his other wrist around as he headed back through the store on his toes. "But hurry, babes, I'm double-parked." Florabelle chased him up the back stairs with a handful of wet moss, while Fedalia pulled the shade over the front door and ran upstairs after them.

As Florabelle put some water into the breakfast coffee and lit the stove Fedalia tied on her apron and started setting the small kitchen table.

"Haven't you got that stage break yet, Gorgeous?" Spart said through a mouthful of graham cracker he'd helped himself to from the cupboard.

"Not just yet, but——"

"But what? Did you ever call up that producer? What's-his-name Gurnell?"

"Well, I didn't think he was the kind, I mean——"

"You mean fresh? Well, so he does paw you here and there. This is only natural. Gorgeous, how many times do I have to tell you to stop putting such a high value on such a low commodity."

Florabelle banged the table with the back of a big measuring spoon. "Now, Spart, you're not being very funny."

"Now wait a minute. Who's trying to be funny? I'm serious."

"Spart Coliss——"

"Never mind Spart, Florabelle," Fedalia said hurriedly. "We've got to get back down to the store in a few minutes, and I want to hear about the agency job and the play. Spart, do you know an agency man named Turner? He's very——"

"Yeah. Very high class. Threllkell's are just a poor imitation of an agency like that. Threllkell and his partners handle what few accounts they have without any hired help, and no brains. Anything to make a sale. The Four A's will probably get 'em someday. But just now that radio is new and has registered so heavy, they're worse than ever. Every one of them thinks he's Jake Shubert or George M. Cohan, and they strike poses all over the joint and 'produce' like mad. At least once a day Threllkell says to Squat, 'Jim, from the twig where I perch——' and Squat says to Halbeard, 'Check with Threllkell and see if he's in our canoe,' and Halbeard says anything that comes into his head just so long as it sounds important. Stuff like 'Everything will be fine if we bracket the show sponsorwise.' But radio is getting so popular it's pretty hard for them to go wrong, no matter what they do. Ah—advertising, advertising——"

"You mean advertising isn't good for anything?"

"I didn't say that at all, Gorgeous dear. I'm only talking about the antics of this one hungry little outfit. Now you take Grantham Turner over at the Turner Agency, for instance. Small, but very high class. He's——"

Fedalia said, "I know Mr. Turner, Spart. I had dinner one night with——"

"Is zat so?"

Florabelle slapped at Spart with a paper napkin. "Spart! Let Fee get in a word, can't you?"

"All right, all right. They say he's quite a guy, this Turner. Heart as big as the moon. A guy like that must be all right and good to do business with. Know what he does? Tips bus boys and out-of-the-ordinary things like that. But this is a pretty big job they're offering me over at Threllkell's, even if they do force a lot of song-and-dance down the people's throats. They specialize in fancy, confusing hokum the public doesn't understand but sometimes buys just out of curiosity."

Fedalia said, "Don't they ever put things in their ads the way people really talk?"

"How do people really talk, lamb-pot?"

"Oh—just simple—and—I guess, honest."

"Not over at Threllkell, Squat, and Halbeard. And maybe you can't blame them when you see the success the picture companies are having with the old P. T. Barnum technique."

"Like what, Spart?"

"Take *The Merry Widow* over here at the Embassy. Do you think this movie could run for nearly a year without the press boys dragging Mae Murray in and out of the Astor Hotel lobby three times a day with the skinniest greyhounds on the most diamond-studded leashes? And the Spectaculars. This picture Great; the next one Very Great; the next one Stupendous——"

"Now, Spart—Fee doesn't know anything about Spectaculars."

"A Spectacular is an oversized twenty-four sheet, a big billboard with lights."

"Isn't *The Merry Widow* a good picture?"

"It's a swell picture, Gorgeous. What's this got to do with it?"

"Well, if every picture has to have a bigger sign and longer words, where will they be ten years from now? Or twenty?"

"They'll still be making bigger signs and longer words. Terrific, maybe, or Colossal, or even Sin-sational, or Sex-sational, or somep'n."

Fedalia said, "When we were kids we put matches on a milk bottle, and after you get 'em built up so high, the matches finally fall off."

"Who can worry about 'after while'? Right now is what

156

pays off, and if the picture across the street cost three million, you gotta say your picture cost four million."

"Do the people keep believing it, though? Maybe someday they'll quit trusting those ads and just stop going to the movies."

"This is where smart advertising comes in. Most of the ad agencies are ethical enough. Only a fly-by-night outfit like T. S. and H. hunt around for overexaggeration and unnatural, stilted language in ads. Get the idea?"

Fedalia nodded. "Then why do you want to work for this Threllkell and—Squat Company?"

"Why not? There's plenty of moolah in it."

Florabelle stopped in front of Spart. "But what about your play, Spart?" she said.

"Didn't I tell you?"

"No, you didn't tell me?" Florabelle imitated her brother, running her voice up into a question. "I haven't seen you but ten minutes in four weeks, remember?"

Spart pulled his sister down on his lap. "I'll tell 'ittle baby sister-kins about buzzer's drate bid play." He poked a kiss at her nose. "Sit still. Remember that semi-pro stock company up in Connecticut I ran across a coupla months ago? Well, I went up there last week to give them some of the new material, and they got the thing in pretty fair shape. Looks like I'll get a tryout up there in a few weeks. Good enough to tell what we got, anyway."

"Good, Spart! Can we go?"

"I should say not. This is the time a guy doesn't want anybody around but strangers and his conscience. How's the flower business, Floozybelle?"

Florabelle stood up and folded her arms. "Well, Brother, the business is going along pretty good. And would you allow me to tell you why? Because I'd like to tell you why, if you're out of breath long enough for me to get a word in here. A while back I was so frazzled with bills I didn't know where to turn to even keep my door open. Now don't laugh, Spart, or I'll hit you over the head with this coffeepot. I started praying one night, see? Now, Spart! You sit there! I started praying in a very random way. Just seeing if I could make a connection. You know, to try to get to the point of feeling that someone was listening to me. Something Fedalia said gave me the idea.

"Well, when I started to ad-lib what I thought I needed, I felt like two cents, taking up time with a whole big thing about the store and some bills here and there. How many people have even got a store—even a busted store—that I should be moaning and groaning as though I really had some tragedy to moan and groan about?

"So you know what I did? I just started to say thanks for the things I had, not the usual routine rigamarol, just thanks in my own words instead of asking for favors. Thanks for my crazy brother, keep him healthy. Thanks for my spot in the world, which is just what I like, and also for my health, and if I can't get out and run this store, I don't deserve to have one and I'm sorry I bothered You. Amen. And we've broken even every day since.

"Now I don't want a word out of either one of you brats. Just you both think it over. Coffee's ready, Fee."

The front doorbell jangled downstairs. Florabelle jumped up and said, "You see? Customers at ten-thirty, yet." She poured some coffee out and took a couple of hurried sips. "Come over to dinner tonight, Spart. I want to hear about your show."

"Maybe. Go ahead, Sis." He looked at his watch. "I'll chew the rag with Gorgeous for a few minutes. Although I don't promise to drink whatever this is you use for coffee."

"Not too long now. Fedalia and I got a wedding to put up

before three. She's on the pay roll now." Florabelle sprinkled her hands in the sink and started down the stairs.

"Ten minutes, Florabelle," Fedalia called after her.

"Okay. Adios, Brother."

"Adios, Fatso." Spart tried the coffee and made a face. "How about Floozybelle discovering prayer through an ad-lib? This is fantastic. Hey, any breaks career-wise, Gorgeous?"

"Helen Jern is looking out for something over at the radio station. She said maybe a group——"

"Well, this is something. You got to be patient, though. Like with my musical. We got a pretty good show put to-gether, I think. Though of course you never know till that first curtain." Spart squinted and bent down over her. "Lemme see you smile, Gorgeous." When she did he kissed her, right on her teeth between her lips.

"That'll teach you to show off your china. Goo'by, baby. I'm off to set'm on their ears at T. S. and H. with the first creative thinking they will ever have had in the joint. See you tonight, if I can get back."

After she heard him clatter down the steps and out the street door Fedalia washed the cups and saucers, put them away, took off her apron, and went slowly down into the store.

CHAPTER TWENTY-FIVE

Fedalia slammed the big icebox door on the morning shipment from the hothouse. Drying her hands on her smock, she leaned against the cutting table and took Spart's letter out of her blouse. It was postmarked Lyme, Connecticut.

Dear Gorgeous:

Here's Number 532 with inside rhymes yet! Ain't it horrible?

> Every day sunrise to sundown
> There's somebody running down
> Love.
> And every evening by the very same token
> Hearts are mended
> That are bent and broken.
> Every night, sundown to sunrise,

Love's dream is a paradise found.
We might as well get on the merry-go-round
Every day.

Bloody, but unbowed—
Invictus

"Fedalia, break it up, girl!"

"I'm sorry, Florabelle. I was——"

"Hurry up. It's Helen Jern on the phone, from ABCA, and she sounds like she's in a rush."

Fedalia ran to the phone back in the store.

"Hello, Helen."

"Listen, Fee. They need a new girl in an octette we use over here on a daytime TC show. It's our first daytime show that goes all the way to the Coast. Can you sight-read?"

"Sight-read, Helen? Well, I don't know how good."

"Never mind. We'll take a chance. Get over here right away."

"Helen! Right now?"

"Whenever it is, you can make it," Florabelle whispered, standing at her elbow.

"I can make it, Helen. . . . I'll come right over. *Thank* you, Helen. G'by! Oh, Helen, does Mr. Wixberry know about it?"

"Not yet. We'll surprise him."

"I'll be there as quick as I can get there, Helen. G'by!" Fedalia grabbed Florabelle's arms. "Florabelle! It's a job at ABCA to sing in an octette. Helen Jern recommended me and they're waiting for me! Florabelle, can I go dressed like this?"

"I'd suggest you take off the smock."

"Well, sure. But I mean is my dress all right?"

"How many costume changes have you got, Alma Gluck? Wash your face and hands good and beat it."

161

The daylight view from ABCA's roof was quite different. She had ten minutes to look at it. After getting accustomed to the new perspective, she began to pick out the opera house . . . and Carnegie Hall . . . and the Park and the Century Theater. And Broadway . . . looking quiet and dignified . . . Mama used to say, "Stay calm and stay dignified, and good and evil will take care of themselves." Nothing evil about New York from here. Or frightening . . . Maybe she'd learn to recognize its beauty down there as well as from up here, like Adelbert said. Looking down at the small buildings on beyond, she tried to make them beautiful, too, but her thoughts kept running back through the avalanche of disappointments that had tried to turn her back.

Maybe now that she actually had a singing job she'd never have to go through anything as hard and confusing as those hated "interviews" that had trip-hammered her puzzled, groggy attempts to stay on her feet. Why had she kept trying over and over? Only that there was something in her that wouldn't let her quit? Like Charlie running the cross-country? Because she wanted to do something for Papa as badly as Charlie wanted to do something for her? Maybe she couldn't have said good-by to Charlie if she had seen him at the depot. Maybe she'd even have given up the New York trip. Maybe that's why Charlie didn't come.

The ten-minute intermission must be over. She mustn't be late her very first day.

Fedalia didn't know anything about musical directors, but she hadn't pictured them as being as nervous and jumpy as Mr. Helb.

"Miss Parker," he said, "you've got to wait with the triplet until after the run in the bass. If you can't feel the phrase, concentrate on the words—wait till 'You belong to me'— count one-AND . . . Then sing the triplet."

162

"I think I can get it right next time, Mr. Helb. . . . I'm sorry."

"And you're sharp in your high register."

Fedalia nodded. She didn't blame him for being out of patience. She was out of patience with herself. Why couldn't she get it right? She'd gone over it often enough. The pianist played the rhythm introduction again and she counted the measures and the beats under her breath, bobbing her head along, even swaying her body to keep track of the time. She came in right with the triplet, but she knew without being told that her voice had that hysterical here-I-go quality Mr. Helb had complained about before.

Just as they started into it again the engineer made a sign through the glass of the control room. "One minute to go," Mr. Helb said nervously. "Now please do your best, Miss Parker." Fedalia watched the clock and felt herself being alternately engulfed up to her throat and drained down to her veins with each jerky advance of the red hand.

Adelbert didn't remember it was Friday till he picked up the day's schedule from his desk.

"Friday? Now, Helen, I positively cannot take auditions today. I positively will not listen to any quivering hopefuls today. And that is double final. Period. What's next?"

"Mr. Wixberry." Helen drew a long deep weary breath. "So many things have piled up here in the last two weeks that every department is frantic. One of the biggest congestions is the list of auditions that have simply got to be heard. By you. Now please, Mr. Wixberry. They've been waiting for you a half hour already."

Adelbert threw a handful of mail at the "in" basket and aimed his chair at the loud-speaker. Helen phoned the audition producer to proceed, and the first of the aural spectacles paraded out through the grid. They were a trio and a dramatic

163

reader. Adelbert nodded at Helen for the report. He glanced at the list. Two down and three to go. He crossed fingers on both hands under his desk. Let them be good. Let them be good.

Two of the three remaining aspirants performed, but with each of their nervous, desperate renditions Adelbert's spirits sank lower and lower till they touched the surface of familiar black swirling, rebellious seas. "That's all, Helen. Tell whoever is left to come back tomorrow, and don't argue."

Helen didn't say a word. As she cut the loud-speaker it automatically switched over to the final number of the scheduled network program. Adelbert gradually became aware of the music.

"Miss Jern!"

"Yes, Mr. Wixberry."

"What, for heaven's sake, is going on in B?"

Helen glanced at her watch. "Sounds like the end of 'Matinee Musical' to me. I'll turn it off."

"Leave it alone!"

Adelbert listened incredulously to the end. "What is going on around here? Am I drunk or crazy? Or is Henry Helb trying to ruin the network or what? Get him on the phone!"

"Mr. Wixberry——"

"Now what are you so jumpy about? Get him on the phone!"

Helen came over to his desk.

"Mr. Wixberry, I wanted to help that poor girl so badly I didn't realize she could be so bad. She was so nervous at the audition, I thought she deserved a chance. In the group. I didn't think——"

"Who? Who? What poor girl?"

"Fedalia Parker. The girl I brought along for Turner that night at the St. Regis."

"Fedalia Parker *sings*?"

"Well, I guess not too well, after what we just heard. I'm sorry, Mr. Wixberry, but she's such a swell kid——"

"You're sorry." Adelbert took out a cigarette and went through the tapping and the lighting with rapid angry movements. He inhaled one puff, then jammed out the burning end in the ash tray. He picked up the phone asking the operator for B studio.

"Henry Helb," he said to the voice on the other end.

"Just a moment, Mr. Wixberry."

Henry Helb said, "Hello, Mr. Wixberry. I hope you didn't happen to hear 'Matinee——' "

"I heard, Helb. Tell the young lady we won't need her after today."

"I told Miss Jern at the time we'd be taking quite a chance, but she thought——"

"I know what she thought. Just let her go, Helb."

"Yes, sir. Should I——"

Adelbert put the phone back in its cradle, got up, and walked over to the big chair in front of his desk. Helen came around to face him as he sat down.

He wondered just how she'd open up on him. He'd never seen her pale and so close to the verge of losing that careful poise of hers. There was even a tremble in her voice as she said, "It seems to me you could have spoken to her yourself, Mr. Wixberry. With a little kindness or diplomacy, at least——"

"Miss Jern——"

The office door interrupted with quick confidence and vigor before he could say any more. He got up quickly.

There was something distantly familiar about the raw-boned, self-possessed, overdressed woman who stood in the doorway.

She brushed past Helen. "Well, well, Dolly Wixberry. As skinny as ever. I'm Lettice Pabalot, third grade."

165

Adelbert stepped across the room. "Why, of course. Mrs. Pabalot—from Fargo. Didn't you send me to the principal's office for whispering one time?"

"Very probably. Now, I'm already late for supper, so I'll come immediately to the point. You're probably a busy man with such a fine office, but never mind that. I happen to have a published piece here, Dolly, that I know you will want to see. Back in Fargo I am chairman of the HHE, the Home, Hobby, and Entertainment Club, and they want this piece given on the radio. Now every time I gave this piece at the club, it was the same thing every time. 'Lettice, that piece ought to be put over! Lettice, that piece has something to it! Lettice, compare the trash on the radio with this piece of yours——' "

"Mrs. Pabalot——"

"*Miss* Pabalot, Dolly, if you don't mind."

"I'm sorry. Miss Pabalot, I'll be glad to turn your composition over to——"

"Fargo is waiting to hear 'Memories of a Daffodil Waltz' put over on the radio, young man, because they consider this piece superior to a lot of the stuff you have on your microphones which, frankly, we don't listen to any too happily back home."

"Well, Miss Pabalot, if you'd care to leave the song——"

"I'd prefer to play it over for you myself, Dolly. After all, the interpretation has something to do with how a piece sounds. I see you have a piano." She handed him a piece of music, and without waiting for an invitation she moved over to the small upright. Adelbert looked at his amazed secretary and back to Miss Pabalot, saw her large hips add the piano bench to their already superb bulk as she removed her gloves, twisted her rings around, flexed her fingers, threw back the lid of the keyboard, and began to sing in a loud, expressionless tone:

"Sing the memories of a Daffodil Waltz, la-la-la
Sing the music that never will halt, la-la-la
With two hearts in June
We will write one sweet rune—
A rune of the moon in June, la-la-la.
The memories of a daffodil will not fall,
So remember the Daffodil Waltz!"

Adelbert cleared his throat as soon as he realized, with relief that there was no second stanza. He said, "Thank you, Miss Pabalot. I'll keep this song of yours, if I may, and pass it on to the music department. I will see that everything is done to find the right program where it might fit in. Rest assured, I will try my best."

"You won't have to try at all, Dolly. If you want a piece that will appeal to everybody, you have it right there in your hand. We'll all be listening back in Fargo. I've just about decided to give up teaching and devote my entire life to song poems, so you may expect more from me as my career unfolds." She stood up. "I'm late, Dolly, but if I get time before going home next week I'll call you. Anyone at home you want me to say hello to?"

"Thank you, but I have no one back there any more. It's been some time, you know."

"I know, and you weren't exactly the most popular kid in town, as I recall. Well, we'll be listening, Dolly. We'll be listening." Miss Pabalot rustled as she went out the door, through Helen's office, and on into the hall.

Adelbert looked at Helen. "Now wasn't that a treat?"

Helen went out to her own office without a word.

"Helen." He went to the door.

"I'll be back, Mr. Wixberry."

"From where?"

"I'm going to the ladies' room if you don't mind."

"I don't mind in the least." Adelbert followed his secretary out the door, across the lobby, and down the hall. "Why didn't you arrange for her to appear on the regular auditions before you took it upon yourself to squeeze her in the back door?"

"Who, Miss *Pabalot?*" Helen didn't slow down as she spoke.

"No, not Miss *Pabalot.* You know who I mean."

"Fedalia did appear on the regular auditions, and you gave her a two-word brush-off over your shoulder from the elevator. Of course Miss Pabalot comes barging in from the home-town plains of Dakota with her intimate knowledge of your boyhood, insults the intelligence of even my tin ear with her ridiculous song, and then gets received like the queen mother."

"Will you allow me——"

"If you follow me in here I'll yell for the police." Helen disappeared into the ladies' room.

Adelbert got another cigarette out of his pocket. Why did he feel it was so vital to justify himself to Helen Jern? His privet-hedge doorstop? Why was he winding up to let her have the whole story? Just how important was this tailored little spitfire to him, anyhow? He'd found out quite a few things already today, and it looked like he was only beginning. This seemed to be the day when his nice strong-minded objective defense against women was crashing around his ears. And Fedalia. Was he in love with an eighteen-year-old girl he'd only seen once in his life? And what was so important suddenly about Helen Jern except as a very functional part of his office furniture? And what did Miss Pabalot and her "Dolly this, that, and the other" have to do——

"Now, Helen . . ." He threw his cigarette quickly into the sand urn at the end of the hall, hurrying back down the corridor as her trim, flying little coattails switched out of the "Ladies" and flicked around the corner. He caught up with her as she threw open her office door. She dropped her bag on the desk and started for the coat rack.

"Big brave man, aren't you?" Her voice clearly revealed held-back tears. "Kicking poor little Fedalia Parkers around all your life, and just—wilting in front of that big Pabalot slob, with her home-town blackmail. Well, I've had just enough——"

She sat down at her desk, opened her bag, and took out a compact. Adelbert stepped behind her, pulled out the chair, picked her up out of it bodily, kicking and squirming, and carried her over to the couch against the wall. There he dropped her without warning. She clutched at her skirt, speechless and outraged.

CHAPTER TWENTY-SIX

"Now sit there and shut up for a minute, will you?"

Adelbert straightened up. "You may want to quit when I get through with what I have to say, but you'll not quit because of old barrel-butt Pabalot and her damned daffodils. If you knew anything about anything, you'd know that false encouragement is the world's deadliest poison. Which is exactly why I fed it to that stupid woman. I would also like you to understand, while we're at it, why I've never in my life made any exceptions in the way I treat the struggling talent and so-called talent around here."

"Including Fedalia Parker. For your information, I——"

"Yes, including Fedalia Parker. And I'd do what I did again, in spite of the—the—mental indigestion that's murdering my insides right now."

"Well, isn't that just too bad!" Helen fumbled for her handkerchief.

"You bet your sweet, dumb, sentimental life it's too bad. And it's a good deal worse than too bad when a girl like Fedalia, whose musical talent you could put in your left eye, manages to filter through and get encouragement in something she has no future in whatever. You'd like me to start handing out a lot of high-flown horse-collar here, there, and the other place, wouldn't you? 'Very nice, Miss Cranberry Junction, very nice indeed. Leave your name for our files, and if anything comes up . . .' That would please you, wouldn't it, Jern? And let's clear everything up while we're at it with respect to a certain young man who jumped off the roof right out here last month. The young fellow with the height-phobia, the boy who wanted to be a singer, Miss Jern, the boy who dashed into my office after murdering 'The Toreador Song' while you were sitting in there with the door shut!"

Helen stared straight up at him.

"You thought he fell, Helen? Well, he very probably jumped."

"Mr. Wixberry! Of all the cold-blooded, rotten——" Helen sprang to her feet.

"Now look here, Helen. If that Toreador kid had said, 'I'll jump off the roof of this building if you don't give me some encouragement about my voice,' I'd have called the police to keep him from jumping, but I would still have had to tell him the truth as I saw it. I refuse to believe truth is evil. If circumstances had piled up behind that boy to the extent that he wanted to take his own life, the damage had been done before he ever walked in here, by the false encouragement injected into his living veins like morphine. Let me ask you. Who killed the dope fiend? The sniveling fools who fed him the junk to begin with? Or the doctor who took it away from him? Any kid could be driven to the same lengths. A kid like Fedalia Parker, thinking she was selling her family short because maybe she wasn't struggling hard enough, blaming herself and everything else, except the fact that she had no talent, being falsely encouraged by everybody-and-his-brother because of her big eyes and her gold hair. If I'd known——"

Helen's angry tears were dry on her face.

Adelbert sat down on the couch, reached for her hand, and pulled her down next to him. "Ever read the biography of a man named Johannes Brahms? The greatest composer of music this or any world ever saw. This Brahms was an introvert, too, Miss Jern, crowded back in on himself. He got that way, everyone will gleefully tell you, after playing for the ladies in a local brothel at the age of nine, because he was scared of little normal girls, among other reasons. Now don't interrupt. I'm going to quiet down here and say what I've got to say. When you get crowded back in on yourself you talk less and observe more, but I feel like talking for once." He slowed down, measuring his words. "Brahms said that the way to *stimulate* talent is to stifle it, strangle it, choke it, ruthlessly and relentlessly. Understand? Look, Helen. There are hundreds of thousands of good kids all over the world, just like Fedalia Parker, who've got a lot of poison star dust in their eyes. Somebody has to be the doctor, has to take the rap. Somebody's got to be concerned enough about their future to be the villain and try to turn them out of a profession in which they can be less than mediocre at the very best.

"And you don't have to worry about ever cutting down somebody who happens to have real talent, either.

"The percentage who have any honest-to-God-given gift, compared to those who are only stage-struck, is maybe one in a million, and you can't drown that one in a million, Helen. They couldn't starve Schubert or browbeat Handel. They couldn't break the spirit of Schumann-Heink or Carrie Jacobs

Bond. They threw Caruso out of the chorus, and they laughed at Chaliapin. You can't stop talent. Real talent is an express train of hurtling, unstoppable iron and steel and steam. You can't derail it. Can't sidetrack it. Talent has one-track courage that thrives on hardships and on unflinching day-in, day-out, soul-wearying, blistering, backbreaking regimes. Ask Anna Pavlova, Ethel Barrymore, Irving Berlin, Paganini, Jenny Lind, Berlioz . . ."

"Mr. Wixberry, I don't know what to say."

"Don't say anything. Fedalia has just that kind of determination, just that kind of one-track courage. And all of it has been misdirected ever since she was a kid. I respect real talent, Helen. That's why I give the kind of comments I do or none whatever, not because I hate talent but because I respect it. And I don't want to take any chances of being misunderstood." He stopped, waiting for Helen to look up. When she didn't, he spoke again. "This idealistic curse of mine has cost me——" He saw Helen look up now, but not at him. He followed her wide shocked eyes to Fedalia standing in the open door of his office.

"I was waiting for you, Adelbert," she said. "I didn't mean to just eavesdrop, but you were talking about me and it was certainly something I know you're glad I heard. Thank you, Adelbert and Helen, ever so much."

She walked out into the hall and closed the door.

CHAPTER TWENTY-SEVEN

An elevator was waiting. Fedalia stepped in, and as the door slammed shut she heard a familiar voice calling, "Down, please." The elevator man stopped the car at the sharp tapping on the door, moved back up to the floor level, opening the door again.

"Gorgeous! Well, this is where I came in. Now don't tell me that's a tear on your face."

"Hello, Spart. No, of course not. I'm so glad to see you."

"Who can I beat up for you today? Of course you'll join me for a cup of tea across the street?"

"I never wanted any before like I do now. I thought you were in Connecticut, Spart."

"That's a short story that may take some time to tell. Let's get set down first. And by the way, what are you doing here?"

"That's pretty long too. It better wait."

They got out of the elevator and hurried across the street,

running, New York style, up the stairs to the chop suey restaurant. They sat down by the Broadway side and were immediately served with the teapot and little cups. Spart ordered a few things and dumped a large tablespoonful of sugar into the pot, stirred it around, and poured.

"If you knew what the matter was, this you could fix," Spart began. "But when you've been working on a show for months, day in and day out with nine other guys, this is not like a lyric, you can't spot the weakness the same way, mainly because you can love a lyric today and then sing it over to-morrow and hate it. But you can't sing over a whole show, and until that first curtain goes up you haven't any idea whether this is a lulu or a turkey. We found out, though, but quick."

"Oh, Spart!"

"Yeah. It's all over. This opening-night routine is worse than anything you can think of, Fee. Even with half amateurs. Everybody took turns going out into the alley to whoops their cookies all day long clear up to the overture."

"Who decided it was a—a—turkey?"

"Well, now that it's all over, we all knew this show was hopeless from the first rehearsal, I guess, but human nature being what it is, you don't admit this and you hang on by your fingernails thinking of the investment of time and money that you've already got in the piece and you insist on seeing it open. At least we had the rare brains to pull it out immediately and quit kidding ourselves."

"Show business is kind of like a sickness, isn't it, Spart?"

"Oh, sure. But you can't do anything about this. You're in show business yourself, Fee, and you might as well face it. Radio, opera, vaudeville, burlesque, county fair, flea circus, it's all show business. Doing something in front of people. Showing them how good you are. Don't sell it short, though, Gorgeous, and don't overlook any part of it, see? Just like a

175

playwright can learn from an amateur performance in Connecticut, a dramatic actress can learn from a singer on the radio, a singer on the radio can learn from a strip-tease gal, and a strip-tease gal can learn from an opera prima donna. It's all the same underneath, entertaining the public, and the technique is basically the same whether you're trying to get them with a high C or a high fanny."

"Spart. Something happened today. . . ."

"Life, liberty, morals, or moonshine, those things are important to a lot of people, but none of that stuff means a thing when you get show business in your blood. It all becomes second fiddle to that applause from out front, and you'll find yourself working no harder for a roar in Madison Square Garden that knocks your hat off than you will for a trickle of drool down foxy grandpaw's chin in the Penny Arcade. Learn all you can in any and all branches every chance you get. Experience, girl, experience. No matter what you have to do to get it."

Yes, Spart, you've told me that before. Many times. Don't put such a high value on such a low commodity, is the way you like to say it.

Spart gulped down a cup of tea, filled it up again, and continued. "But that's enough about you for a while. Now I got a little something to tell about me." He waved his hand in an airy circle. "I'm finally in the agency business, lass."

"Oh, Spart——"

"The high-and-mighty advertising business. The business that is taking over show business so fast that Princeton has added a rouge, eye-shadow, and crepe-hair course to their commercial-law curriculum."

"Spart, I hope not at that firm with the crazy name?"

"Well, it's rather a long and involved story——"

"Spart . . ."

"You see, Jim Squat is an old friend of mine, Gorgeous.

I was kidding around with some new-style commercials one day and he got really excited about this——"

"I know, Spart, you told me——"

"Well, he kept at me to give T. S. and H. exclusive control of my brain children. Well, I was playing hard to get, see? Meanwhile he came up to Connecticut to catch our turkey. Naturally we got plastered together after the debacle, and just to keep my mind off that miserable flop I got to razzing Jim about his revolting name, and somehow or other my real name came out in the conversation."

"Your real name?"

"Give me some courage, Gorgeous. Haven't you got some Zenobia Undercouplings in your family? Or a Charles W. Horsebottom or something?"

Fedalia smiled. "Spart, I am the great-granddaughter and namesake of La Australia del Espiritu Santo Parker!"

"God be praised!" Spart yelled out, and hammered the table till the dishes jumped. "My name is Coliseum!"

"I don't believe it!"

"True! True! So help me, it's true. Ask Florabelle. My folks were a little self-conscious about such a magnificent moniker and they changed it two weeks after they arrived here from Athens. But can you imagine what this sound did to a fellow with the name of Jim Squat? Can't you see him staring out into space with glassy eyes, huh, Fee? Just a-rolling his tongue around this noble high-sounding name? Well, anyhow, he promised to stump for a junior partnership for me if I'd change my name back like it was, and the minute I got off the train I beat it over to take him up on it. Threllkell, Squat, Halbeard, and Coliseum! Is this something?"

"I guess it is, Spart. But after what you told me about that firm——"

"That's only half of it. You got to admit Jim's offer was a very tempting how-do-you-do-I'm-sure. But just as I started to reach for the dotted line, my one good eye, the one with the principles in it, saw red."

"You saw what?"

"That's 'ee old straight man, old-girl-old-socks-old-keed. I mean I saw gooms. Red luscious gooms on the sign over Jim Squat's desk which said DOWN WITH DECAY THE GAMBIT WAY—THRICE-A-DAY THE POWDER WAY.

"Well, aside from the insult of rhyming way with way, any half-wit would recognize that if you brush your teeth 'thrice a day' you're doing the best thing in the world for your choppers regardless of what you put or do not put on your brush. It's like the old Indian snake oil: 'Take half a teaspoonful as directed with a gallon of water. Guaranteed to stimulate tired and sluggish kidney action.' Well, I hope to tell you, you're gonna get action with all that water. But even in the days of the Mighty Medicine Man the sheriff was always right around the corner trying to help the sucker get half a break. Over at Threllkell's, however, they got the idea to put the fantastic claims in poetry. That's poetic license. It's a great idea, but it's dynamite in the hands of an unscrupulous outfit like T. S. and H."

Fedalia took her chin off her palm, discovered her wrist so cramped from her concentrated listening position she had to waggle it carefully a few times to get the crick out of it. "You mean you can say things that aren't true just because it's poetry?" she said.

With his left hand over his heart and his right hand pointing to the ceiling Spart recited:

"From the Horn to Nova Scotia, from Japan to Turkey, yessir.

"You will never find the equal of Finnegan's Fancy Home Economy, large, medium, and small portable pants presser."

"Spart. That's not poetry."

"Oh no? It rhymes on the ends, and that's enough to permit you to tell the world that your portable pants presser has no equal anywhere in the entire Western Hemisphere, to say nothing of the East and Near East. Now, if you can get away with all that misrepresentation in broken-down couplets, think what you could say in song jingles and musical limericks. Hm?"

"So what did you tell Mr. Squat?"

"I told him I'd let him know and I went across the street and two blocks down to Granthum Turner's agency, who handles a big toothbrush account, and besides that, he has the reputation for being an honest all-round good Indian. Tips bus boys, can you imagine? And does crazy warmhearted things like that, they say, every time he turns around."

"I know, Spart. I——"

"Anyhow, I walked out on Jim."

"Oh, Spart. Why did you string it out so?" Fedalia dropped back in her chair with a relieved sigh.

"Took a bit of walking, I don't mind saying, when I saw the painters already at work on the front door with Threllkell, Squat, Halbeard, and Coliseum. And believe me, that walk was strictly out of character, Gorgeous. I just naturally ain't that noble, but I had been struck someway or other with a hunk of lightning that made me want to sell a product on its merit even if it was only a toothbrush. And Granny Turner signed me up, with all my little jingles, and I ain't no V.P., but I'm an all-fired account executive with a good stiff brush."

Fedalia put out her hand. "Congratulations! And I'm real proud of you, Mister Account Executive, without even knowing what that is."

Spart pulled her hand across the table and pushed back his chair, putting his left foot expansively on his right knee.

"Thanks, lass, thanks. I deserves your kind commendation. Now what's with you?"

"I'm afraid——"

"Seriously, lamb-pot, my commercial gimmicks have so far been all musical, but I got some dramatic ones up my sleeve too. The musical ones are, you know, with singers, maybe two boys and a girl, but we may be five or ten years ahead of the times for jingle commercials, so I'm going to try some dramatized ones just in case, and as soon as I dope out something with a speaking part I'll suggest you. It'll be any day now, the way Turner is eating up everything I suggest. The—— Hey, what's the matter?"

Fedalia had taken her hand away from his. Dropping her eyes, she sat back in her chair. She didn't see how she could answer.

"Hey, Gorgeous. What gives here?" He snapped his fingers in front of her face. "Wake up, girl, wake up."

"Spart . . . Didn't you even know I was a singer?"

"A singer, Gorgeous? Well, now that you—that is, someway I always got it in my head you were trying for dramatic roles—you know, those daytime things. . . . You mentioned Helen Jern trying to get you on a daytime radio show, didn't you? I got the impression——"

"And here all the time you didn't even know I was a singer. Spart, didn't you hear me tell you about opera being my biggest ambition ever since I was thirteen years old?"

"Gorgeous, I don't know how I got so mixed——"

"I guess, come to think of it, it doesn't make any difference now."

It was strange to see Spart embarrassed, looking at her so helplessly. She said, "I've learned a lot about show business, though. I'll just go on home now while you're waiting for the bill——"

"Fedalia, wait a minute."

"No, really. I'd rather go on. Thanks for the tea, Spart."

Fedalia picked up her coat and went out of the restaurant, down the stairs to Broadway up through Times Square.

She walked slowly, making no effort to keep pace with the thoughts rapidly crowding in, crowding in. How had she ever gotten so mixed up? *Why? Why?* What sense had there ever been to her bewildered treadmill efforts to be something or somebody she hadn't really wanted to be at all? Where was Fedalia Parker? Who was Fedalia Parker? She was not a singer, for one thing, that was clear enough.

Fedalia Parker, non-singer. She was also Fedalia Parker, ex-New Yorker. She belonged back in Fort Madison taking care of the boys. Maybe Mr. Quimby would give her a job in the greenhouse again, a full-time job.

Fedalia Parker, old maid. Charlie would certainly have forgotten her by now. The tears were trying to come, smarting and paining her lids.

Fedalia Parker, old maid. She'd just take right up where she left off. Nobody at home had ever seen her even have a date with a boy.

"I know a genius when I see one." Do you, Papa?

"Your *bel canto* is solid, my dear, basic, intuitive; you'll go far, my little bird." Now Mrs. Wilmert. And Spart, oh, Spart, what a fake. A wonderful, nice, fascinating, sweet fake. But you ought to listen to what you say sometimes, Spart. You ought to listen to those smart sophisticated things you say and then forget about, Mr. Coliss. They are very convincing. They send girls out to gather up emotional experiences from somebody like Tom Gurnell. And you, Jess, and you, Ernie, and Helen and Florabelle. Couldn't anybody hear? Couldn't anybody see?

If they could, they didn't have the courage to pull out the truth and look at it. But that's what you said, Adelbert, about my blaming everything else except that I have no talent. You

181

told the truth that very first day at ABCA, Adelbert. You told the truth about the way I sang in the octette, and you told the truth to Helen today. Me and my Iowa stubbornness and my one-track courage—all headed in exactly the wrong direction! And you were the only one who tried to set me straight. Fedalia Parker, old maid. That'll be me, Adelbert. You're a real important person and the bravest person I know, next to Charlie. All those wonderful things you explained to Helen Jern. They ought to be in a book someplace and you ought to be President and I ought to go back home and start over.

And now she could say good-by to the group of assorted tall people she'd met so often in her dreams, tall people like the ones in the serious cartoons in the evening paper. Tall thin wandering men and women huddled around a crossroads sign with pointing arms, always being directed firmly and with great authority by other men and women to the different highways, pleasantly and engagingly. "Leave your name and address, and if anything comes up," they were always saying. I'm one of the lucky ones. I'm getting another chance. I'm back at the crossroads sign again and I'm taking the right fork this time.

She felt tired all through when she tapped on the door of the flower store just as Florabelle was pulling down the north blind.

"Fee, pet! Come in fast and tell me, tell me, tell me. Did you sing?"

Fedalia threw off her coat and dropped down onto the edge of the show window. "Florabelle, if you're all through for the day can we go upstairs? I don't think I'm going to cry or anything like that, but I'd sure like to put on an apron and help you get supper and tell you what happened."

Florabelle pulled her to her feet. "Well, you just know

it. Come to Auntie Flo, baby, and spill it all out, with tears or without."

Fedalia wanted to let go in the comfort of Florabelle's big warm hug, but she didn't. This was no stopping point. It was actually a beginning, and that's not the time to cry. New York hadn't made her cry yet, and she wasn't going to give in today.

Together they went up the back stairs. Fedalia got her apron from back of the door and started setting the table.

"Florabelle, I can't sing. Never could. It was all a big mistake, right from the beginning. I might have known it, if Papa hadn't wanted it so badly. I don't want to tell all the details just now, about today. Helen was there and she could tell you sometime. The main thing is I found out I can't sing worth anything. And even though I was really shocked about it all, I know it's good that I found out, and if I could stay here with you tonight, I'll go over to Uncle George in New Jersey tomorrow and borrow some money I need to get back home where I should never have left. I can work in the greenhouse and take care of the boys."

Florabelle had dropped into the kitchen chair while Fedalia was talking. "Fee, honey, I had an instinct about it the whole time. But you shouldn't be too hard on all of us, dear. You know you sure do look the part. Spart is dead right when he calls you 'Gorgeous' all the time. You are, inside and out."

"Florabelle, you've been so good to me. And Spart——"

"Spart did fine, for him. Of course I knew from the start he was going to come as near to loving you as he could anybody. And I also know that in the middle of his good behavior he has been storing up a happy time for himself with you in his one-way mind. Well, you go home, Fee. Back to Fort Whatyoumacallit. Spartan's too late. You're going to get out of your system all the heartbreak of this town and the show-offs and the—the——"

She got up and started noisily setting the table. "And if necessary I'll put the Federal Bureau of Investigation on his trail to keep him from showing up at the station when you leave town. This is one third-act curtain he ain't gonna write. You're not for show business, Fee, and you're not for Spart Coliss."

"Now wait a minute, Florabelle. Spart never——"

"Now you wait a minute. I've heard him sit around this very flat filling you with advice about show business that didn't fit you any more than the flower business fits him. Show-business people can talk that way to each other and understand a lot of unsaid stuff in between the lines. They all understand that the curtain is up practically all the time whenever any of them opens his mouth. They expect to show off in front of each other and they like it. It's more that than a two-way code of morals. I don't think they actually believe there's one code for show people and one code for everybody else, but that's just about what he told you, Fedalia, every time you were with him. Didn't he now? And he's pretty believable, Fee."

"Florabelle . . . Spart didn't even know I was a singer." Fedalia thought she was starting to laugh, then she had to bite her lip to keep from crying. It was twice as hard not to, with Florabelle's arms tightly around her.

CHAPTER TWENTY-EIGHT

There was a dirty little glass window on the firebox, and the thick red paint around it was starting to peel. There was also a series of hastily scratched initials on the paint. Initials were always hastily scratched on fireboxes, Adelbert thought, as though it were a real daring exploit to fool around with public property like that. Some people have a queer conception of what's brave and daring. Look at me. Here I am back behind this firebox waiting to catch a glimpse of a little Iowa girl I can't get out of my head. That seems rather daring to me. At least I'm furtive enough about the whole idiotic performance to be Jimmy Valentine picking the lock on the vault of the United States Mint. And profligate. Am I profligate with the time of day. I've squandered enough hours during this watch to have learned bookbinding, gem cutting, Sanskrit, Gregg's shorthand, and the Australian crawl, and unless I'm beginning to see things, there's somebody giving me a surreptitious once-over from behind that lamp-post across the street and slightly down the block.

It's unusually dark and shadowy in this street, and deserted too. At this hour of the night everybody is out someplace at a movie, I suppose, or gone early to bed. There won't be any goings and comings around here for an hour or so. Then why am I expecting to see Fedalia at this hour? Well, she doesn't answer the buzzer. She's got to come home sometime, and coincidence is a funny thing, no respecter of logic.

There certainly is somebody watching me from behind the lamppost. . . . Hmmmm . . . The last thing in the world I would enjoy would be investigating whoever it is, so just as a matter of sheer character discipline I expect I'm in for it. Being afraid has nothing to do with being a coward, I think. Well, the sooner I sneak up on that guy, the sooner I'll find out that he's some kid sneaking out of the house for a go at a Sweet Caporal or a Cubeb. . . . Or else he's not a guy at all but a shadow. Hmmm . . . It's a guy all right. . . . Hmmmmmm . . . Well, here we go then. First we slip away from the firebox into the shadow of this convenient stoop, then quietly we retreat, door-to-door fashion, a safe distance down the block. . . . Maybe I could get arrested for this. . . . Now that telephone pole throws a nice black shadow on the hock shop right across the street. I could easily cross, completely unseen, right over that shadow, providing I go on my toes; there's such a damn echo in this empty block. . . . Feel like a damn toe dancer. . . . The idea is not to worry about being scared, Dolly, my boy. Everybody is scared. The idea is to do it even if you are scared. . . . Okeh then, I hope you're satisfied—here we are on the same side of the street, me and my shadow friend. . . . Door-to-door, tiptoe technique again will do it, I guess, if I can just keep back out of the feeble radius of that lamppost. . . . Yeah, it's a guy all right—a pretty big guy, huddled up in his overcoat. He'd hear me if it wasn't for the distant racket over there on the avenue. . . . Oh-oh, there goes a siren down the next street. Much obliged, Mr. Fire Commissioner. That will give me time to be right on this lad before he even dreams I'm here. . . . Now then, I'll yell good and loud.

"Say, you! What are you——"

Adelbert threw himself into his surprise approach with such furious abandon that he slipped on both feet and dropped like he was shot, striking the curbing with his head on the way down.

Fedalia used to like to go to an early movie, if she went, Spart Coliss thought, and I know she's not home yet because she doesn't answer the buzzer. If she went to a movie she might be coming home about now. Why did I let her walk out on me, anyhow?

I'll just nicely stand here behind this lamppost and keep an eye on her flat for one more half hour, don't ask me why. This Iowa nasturtium worries me or something. . . . Holy catfish, I'm sure wasting a lot of time standing around on this street. In the hours I've frittered away doing this I could have read the complete works of Shakespeare, mastered contract bridge, translated the biography of Rimsky-Korsakov, and carved a mahjong set out of the jawbone of an East Indian ass, and am I starting to see things, or is this a guy over behind that firebox giving me the hinge? Hmm . . . There's sure something or somebody over there behind that firebox, just standing there. . . . Hmmm . . . I could sneak over there and—— Hey, Coliss, are you crazy or something? Want to get your head bashed in by some mug maybe all hopped up? Prob'ly my imagination, anyway. . . . Well, let him stand there, this is okay with me. . . . He's wasting a lot of time. . . . At least I'm a lyric writer, I can dream up a little something here, don't need any equipment but my

187

nimble brain. Don't even need a pencil and paper. Any lyric that's worth the powder to blow it up can be remembered the first time through, at least by the author. . . . Let's see what lyrics have I got tucked away that I never finished. . . . "Ev'ry day, sure as the sunrise . . ." Hmmm, this is funny. I can't see that bird at all now. . . . Well if he left I'd certainly have heard his footsteps—with the hollow echo on this street you could hear a gnat trudging off to his evening shift in the sewer. . . . Funny how New York has this constant dull sound off in the distance all the time, and there goes the good old fire department down toward the avenue. They say San Francisco has the loudest fire department in the world. Well, brother, it's got to go some to——

A loud voice came from close behind him: "Say, you! What are you——" Spart felt his blood run cold as he barely managed to dodge two big feet that came leaping up out of no-place. He was pleased to notice their owner chip out a loose piece of the curbing with his head on the way down. In another moment he was dumfounded to find himself trying to revive—of all people—A. B. Wixberry!

Adelbert came to quickly and sat up, feeling like a cross-legged Buddha incense burner as he looked at the young man bending over him with plain bewilderment. "How do you do," Adelbert said. "Didn't you knock me down once before?"

The young man cleared his throat. "If you are Adelbert Wixberry, masticator of singing women and children, yes, I am comparatively proud to say, yes, I did knock you down on an earlier occasion, but your implication that I also knocked you down here just now is a mistaken one. You, in fact, almost knocked me down, with both feet, an attempt which, I am pleased to point out, invariably unhorses the kicker as well as the kickee, and your prone position on the asphalt just now testifies loudly that the recent demonstration was no exception. Not to mention the admirably imposing egg that is beginning to rise into considerable prominence on the outer casing, or shell, of what you no doubt affectionately refer to as your brain."

"Well, then, it appears that you are still one up on me. By your leave, sirrah, since we're being so bookish and lit'ry . . ." And Adelbert reached back for a soul-satisfying roundhouse flailing swing that caught the young man right on the button. Back over he went, leaving Adelbert still sitting in the street with all the dignity and bearing he could possibly muster. *Now this is quite a feeling!*

His surprised victim wearily pulled himself up to his feet. With a grin he reached down and boosted Adelbert upright also. "A fair thing's a fair thing, Wixberry. Do we start now from scratch?"

Adelbert stuck out his hand. "Okeh. Coliss, I believe your name is. There's my five."

"Okeh, Wixberry, let's go get a cup of coffee."

"Not dramatic enough, Coliss. I thought you were a writer. We will walk over to ABCA, where in the third drawer on the left-hand side of my desk is a bottle of *pre*-war Dewars with which we will end *this* war! How's that for a lyric?"

"Lousy! When will you amateur poets learn that words which sound alike don't rhyme with each other, but everything else you said is so poetic it makes my head swim. Let's go, Slugger!"

They finished the Dewars and scattered lily cups all over the office as well as increasingly unintelligent observations. Adelbert admitted he had been waiting for Fedalia. Sort of a big-brother-happened-to-be-passing-by-and-was-worried-about-the-poor-kid kind of thing.

"That's exactly why I was there," Spart confessed.

In the meantime the Dewars was making each explanation more labored and involved.

When they finally left, the night elevator was locked up and they had to walk down thirty-nine flights.

CHAPTER TWENTY-NINE

Fedalia rattled the screen with her knocking, but it was plain by this time that Uncle George was not at home. She wondered why he kept the screen on the year round. He was so methodical about so many other things. She knocked again. It must be nearly three. He could be at his office downtown at this hour of an afternoon. Maybe Miss Broder at the rooming house would know where the office was. Fedalia went back along the narrow walk and started toward the end of the block. She mustn't forget to observe Uncle George's wish about concealing her identity from his sister as long as she could do it honestly.

She bent over to pick up a little flat curved leaf from the sidewalk. It was faded and dry. Back in Fort Madison the same little leaves dropped on their front walk. In the summer when they were green and fresh you'd fit them on your tongue right where you say "Dee," then stub your tongue against that leaf in just the right way and it would honk just like a duck. Your tongue tickled with the vibration.

She turned down the walk leading to the big shapeless house. She certainly didn't look forward to seeing Miss Broder with her suspicious way of refusing any kind of friendly remark. The metal pipe railing leading up through the leaves to "her" room was rusty and sagging in the daylight. As she started to press the front doorbell Miss Broder came around the side of the house. A man's brown sweater, buttoned high up around her neck, was hanging down to where her short legs began. The two sweater pockets sagged below her waist, one dirty furnace glove stuffed in each. She stopped a few feet from Fedalia and squinted her eyes. "What do you want?" she said.

"Hod-a-do, Miss Broder. I'm——"

"I know who you are. What do you want?"

"Miss Broder." Fedalia stretched her wrist out of her sleeve. "I could feel goose-pimples coming out on my skin just from being nervous of you. You can see them, can't you, Miss Broder? When I was little I used to be very nervous of Mr. Woodhouse down by the bridge—because he always growled at children. Not that you growl, exactly, Miss Broder."

Miss Broder's eyes opened wide.

"You only squint to frighten people because you're frightened of them, really. Like we found out about Mr. Woodhouse."

Miss Broder pulled one long sweater sleeve out over her grimy hand. Then she turned and started down the narrow walk at the side of the house.

Fedalia walked along after her. "You wouldn't be frightened of people any more at all, Miss Broder, if you would just be polite and stop trying to make them think you are fierce inside. I think you're kind inside, and now that I said it, I'm not afraid of you at all. Could I have a drink of water, please, Miss Broder? I only stopped in to ask if you could direct me to your brother's office."

Fedalia had been following Miss Broder around the corner of the house, talking to her back. When she mentioned Uncle George's office, the back stiffened as Miss Broder stopped short, then turned around slowly.

"What do you know about my brother?" she said. Her voice was so low Fedalia had to strain to hear it.

"Why, I've known Mr. Broder since I first came to West Guage. In fact, he asked me about doing some errands for him in New York. He sent me to your rooming house, you know. And now I have to see him on business. If you don't know where his office is, I expect I could find the address in a directory or at the City Hall or——"

"I'll get you the water," Miss Broder interrupted. Fedalia followed her to the back steps. In a few moments she came back through the kitchen door with a heavy red glass and a paper napkin. "Care for a napkin?" she said, offering the glass.

Fedalia said, "Thank you ever so much. Isn't that a pretty glass, though?"

"You'll notice 'St. Louis World's Fair' scrolled on there. I was there on my—— I was there. Nineteen ought four."

"It's very pretty." Fedalia drank the water and patted her mouth with the napkin. "Thanks ever so much," she said.

"You don't have to go to the City Hall," Miss Broder said. "Dr. Broder's office is down at Third and Front over the wallpaper store."

"Doctor Broder?"

"When I first come to West Guage he called himself doctor. He left town then for several years, and when we come back he never called himself doctor any more."

"You went with him?"

"Oh yes. He never give me much company, but he's all

the kin relative I got. Had a sister, but she died a good many years ago. You're a sweet young one to put up with me, even to stand here talking."

Fedalia smiled. "I liked you right off, Miss Broder, even though you frightened me at first."

"Well, it's just that I don't have much to say, and then I guess I just got to mistrusting everybody. I can talk to you, though. I'll go with you down to George's office."

"I couldn't let you do that, Miss Broder. I'm in quite a hurry. I'm sure I can find it. Thank you, Miss Broder. I'm sorry if I——"

"Did he ever tell you what happened to his wife?"

"Why, yes, he told me. She died four months ago."

Miss Broder took hold of Fedalia's arm. "There's something about George, miss. I'd ought to tell you——"

Fedalia started to back off into the driveway leading out to the street. "Miss Broder, excuse me for interrupting, but I'm in such a hurry. The thing is, I'm going back home where I live in the Middle West, today, if possible, and I have to see him about the train today, too, and it's such a real long trip. I know your brother is very odd, but that's just his way, and I have to see him before I go. I—— Good-by, Miss Broder. Everybody has their odd ways, I guess. Thanks ever so much." Fedalia started half running along the drive, kept going straight across the street. As she turned to follow the sidewalk up to the corner toward town, she waved back at the brown sweater and the short legs waiting by the front steps. The paper napkin answered the wave, held awkwardly aloft.

Fedalia slowed down somewhat after she got to the next corner where the stores began. A man selling chestnuts hovered over his little peanut stove. The way he bundled and huddled up to the small glow made Fedalia realize the sharp chill in the air. He told her they were on First Street—

then came Second, then Third, and Front was two blocks more, to the left.

She started hurrying again, partly from chill and partly from anxiety. Anybody who ever talked to Uncle George would have to admit he was odd. People all start acting this way or that way when they're children, and whichever kind of acting appeals to them, they exaggerate more and more as they grow up. This one becomes stiffer, that one becomes quieter, or louder, or shyer, or crueler. Like the favorite colors people wear . . . He wears mostly green; she wears only light colors, or only red, or only yellow, but each is sure his color is the thing to make him stand out from everybody else. Uncle George would have been a small unnoticed child—quiet— but how do you get people to notice you when you're quiet? How do you become superior? People would notice you all right if you were quietly cruel—like so many children are cruel. And then that gets to be your favorite color and you wear it and wear it, and when you're grown up the play acting has become you. But she had no real reason to think Uncle George was actually cruel, had she?

The glass show window of the wallpaper store had been broken for some time, the way it looked. It was pasted together down the break with wrapping paper and a diagonal board propped from one side to the other. The store had been closed, too, for some time, it looked like.

It was a very small building, and the steps that led up from the sidewalk were narrow and dirty. Uncle George had no business sign of any kind on the wall or anywhere she could see. She went up the stairs to the second floor, each step stirring up a lazy puff of stale dust.

The two doors in front were padlocked and silent. In the rear one door stared open, showing a small yellowish lavatory with a brown stripe streaking up the side of the bowl to the faucet that ended an angleless pipe sticking straight out from the wall. The door directly opposite was half glass, thick and frosted. It was scratched badly in the center part as though to remove the letters of a name. There was a faint light burning beyond the door. Fedalia tapped as politely as she could on the glass. Instantly the light went out, almost as though it had been wired to her rapping. She rapped again and called out, "Uncle George. It's me, Fedalia." The door opened suddenly. The only surprise on her uncle's face came from his eyes.

"Come in, Fedalia. Come in. Well, I've wondered about you." His sleeves were half rolled up. One rubber-gloved hand held an inside-out glove he must have just stripped off. His thick shoulders looked even thicker without his coat on. He reached overhead, pulling a cord attached to a ceiling bulb which dimly lit the small room, empty except for a hall tree near the door and a stiff brown-and-black leather couch against the wall. There was a room beyond, visible only because of the thin frame of light around the shade rolled down against the window. She took a few steps into the room as Uncle George closed the door behind her.

"I'm glad to see you, Uncle George," she said. "Miss Broder told me where to come. I should have written you more, but I—we—my whole career was a mistake—my singing and all. I really don't have enough talent to stay on—I mean any talent. I've planned to go back home to Fort Madison. Right away. I belong there, Uncle George, and I'm not sorry about it because now I've got so many things straight in my head that I was mixed up about before. I'm sure you must be busy."

"Not at all, my dear." He made his suggestion of a forward bow. "My work is exacting, but it takes patience and much —much—time. I'm philosophical about interruptions. Unfinished work lends anticipation to the ultimate completion. In a similar way, although I missed seeing you, I nevertheless basked in the anticipation of your return, which somehow I felt satisfied was inevitable. Fated, shall we say?"

"Well, you are my only uncle," Fedalia said nervously. "I hope you won't think it's the wrong thing for me to ask you to loan me twenty-five dollars, Uncle George. Now that I've got things straightened out, I just feel I'm marking time in the wrong part of the world. The boys need me and I need them—and—home. . . . I could pay you back in a very short time. I have nearly forty dollars, and the twenty-five would make enough for my railroad fare."

"Why, yes, of course, Fedalia, if you're sure you want to go home. But there's really not that much hurry, is there? Even if I had a thousand nieces, my dear, I'm sure you would always be my favorite. I'd like you to stay for a while—with me. Now that you have no interest in your career, I'd like to project mine for those sympathetic eyes and ears of yours. You have a great talent, my girl. Maybe not for music, but certainly for understanding. . . . There's much you don't understand that I want to teach you." His thin lips parted with the rapid transforming of his thoughts into short, clipped syllables, coming faster and faster.

"Uncle George, I can't stay any longer. I get frightened of you sometimes, the way you talk—like you're deliberately—doing it. . . ."

"My career is the science of pain, Fedalia. I study it slowly and carefully. But it's real intensities unfold to the full only when other eyes are looking over my shoulder. . . . Horrified eyes at first, you know? But always fascinated." His words crowded stickily through his dry, nervous mouth and his breath was short. He stepped quickly behind Fedalia and actually threw the brown leather couch sideways across the door in one motion of his short arms. It crashed heavily on the floor. "You'll have to leave by the other door."

Fedalia pushed her way past him into the inside room,

realizing almost as she did so that there couldn't be any other door but the one she had just been tricked into going through. Uncle George followed quickly, closing the door behind them, turning the flat key in its lock, slipping it into the palm of his rubber-gloved hand. He turned a wall switch, and a green-shaded desk lamp with a half-globe metal shade shone down on the narrow chest-high table. A series of black elastic strips laddered along the table top, tightly fastened underneath. Under two of the strips was Raggy. Its small round eyes stared big from straining against the pressure on its throat, the pupils contracting with terror at every movement in the room.

"Uncle George!" Fedalia stopped her own whispered cry with the hand her horrified reaction had flung up against her mouth.

"Oh, it's quite logical and scientific." His voice was soft, the words clipped. "Raggy came to my door of her own accord the day I returned home in the rain from the funeral of my beloved Bernette. Just a drenched rag of a guilty little cat, as though it had walked all the way from the cemetery. Bernette understood me and my studies. You see, Fedalia?

"Then she developed her illness and died just before your father's letter came along. It seemed a long time before you finally came. But the months went by, and I never really minded the waiting. Besides, Raggy was here to remind me I wouldn't be alone for long—sent, I feel sure, by my beloved Bernette the day she was buried, though the cat nevertheless came all that way from the cemetery of its own accord.

"And then you came. Just like Raggy, of your own accord. And when you left I knew you'd come back. Of your own accord." Uncle George looked at her with small burning eyes. Fedalia had never before felt the kind of fright that wouldn't let her move or think.

"You see, Fedalia? It's only your imagination that horrifies

198

you. You were nearly too late for Raggy. We may find, however, that you yourself could easily learn to embrace pain —either to receive it or to inflict it. . . . It's a science, my dear, deep and profound."

Fedalia dropped her hands limply to her sides. She had to get Raggy off the table. Being afraid has nothing to do with being a coward, she said over to herself. I can be as afraid as I want and still get Raggy off that table.

He was saying, "And remorse is not scientific, my dear. I'll show you. You see, without the scientific witness—or better, the partner—my solitary experiments are a form of self-abuse, as you might say—that is——"

"Uncle George . . ." Fedalia went over to the table. The cat's cry was hoarse and small when she loosened the tight straps over its throat and its body. Raggy dug into Fedalia's coat with frantic claws.

"I'm going home now. You won't hurt me or keep me here. As sorry as I am for Raggy, I'm even sorrier for you. Most children pull wings off of flies and cut angleworms in two, but they get over it when they change from cruel little animals into people. They learn to want to show off to their parents and to the other kids instead of showing their power over angleworms and flies. And then they learn to show off to themselves, which is the best of all because that means doing something for somebody else. There are a lot of things I don't understand about you, Uncle George, but I'm sure you're not satisfied with the things you do, even if you don't know about remorse, as you said. I don't know if you're what you'd call crazy or not—or what makes you like you are. Personally, I think you've got about the same things in you that everybody else has, except way too much of some and not nearly enough of others. You want to be the one people like or respect or fear—if not people, animals will have to do. You're an animal, Uncle George—a cruel little animal—and you'll stay that way until you show off to yourself just once. Did you ever do one good thing for anybody in your whole life? You'll really feel important then. Give me the key, Uncle George. . . ."

Uncle George's rubber glove made a wet squeaking sound as he pulled it off. His face was dripping perspiration, but he appeared not to realize it, making no attempt to wipe it off. He backed over to the narrow table; then, ignoring Fedalia, with Raggy squirming desperately in her arms, he appeared to be examining, almost fondling, the two loose elastic strips. As she watched his fumbling fingers he dropped the strips abruptly and turned toward her again, holding up the key. She moved closer to him, gripped Raggy tightly with one arm, and reached out, taking the small bit of metal from his hand. She backed across the room till she felt the doorknob behind her, then bent down, half turning till she could fit the key in the lock. . . . Slowly straightening up, she opened the door.

Uncle George pushed past her without warning—threw himself down on the leather couch in the outer office, looking up at her and away with quick darting movements of his small eyes. Fedalia was breathing quickly, feeling her heart pound quickly, too, against Raggy's little body.

Heavy, anxious steps—noisy with urgency—pounded up the hall stairs. Uncle George's head turned sharply, his small startled eyes moving in jerky panic from Fedalia to the barricaded door behind him, to the light cord hanging down from the ceiling, to the dimly lit room beyond. The sound of the steps reached the landing. Uncle George got quickly to his feet and started toward the inner office. As he did so Fedalia slipped behind the couch and forced one end of it out into the room. It was Miss Broder who threw open the door at that moment.

200

"Bernette!" Uncle George spoke the word in a whisper, but with a violence that carried it unmistakably to Fedalia's shocked brain. The tall gray-suited man accompanying Miss Broder, severely normal in every aspect of his appearance, gave Fedalia the only assurance that any of this could possibly be happening.

Uncle George spoke again, quietly this time, and slowly, raising dull, focusless eyes to his wife's face. "So you told them, Bernette. . . . Well . . . I suppose you had to some-day."

The tall man stepped over to Uncle George. "I want you to come with me, Mr. Broder," he said. "We can get any of your things later."

"Why, yes, of course." Uncle George showed his short gray teeth in a polite smile. "Certainly." He reached out to take his brown coat and small brown hat from the hall tree. Miss Broder moved across the room to help him into the coat. He put it on, hooked it carefully down the front. In doing so the rubber gloves he had in his hand fell to the floor with a soft plop of sound. The tall man, ignoring the gloves, took Uncle George's arm.

At the door Uncle George turned back, completely self-assured once more. "You're quite right about showing off, Fedalia. Most good deeds strike me as exhibitionism, you know? But showing off to yourself. Now I never quite thought of that." He reached awkwardly into the inside pocket of his coat with his left hand. Taking out a thin cloth wallet, he took from it—one at a time—five five-dollar bills and handed them to Fedalia. "And now I'm supposed to feel important, hmm? Well, we'll see. We'll see." He lifted the angled couch from one end without any apparent effort and let it fall in the middle of the small room. He continued to stand there in the small cloud of dust curling up from the floor, making just a suggestion of a forward bow as Fedalia said, "Thank you, Uncle George," and went out to the stairs, holding Raggy tightly against her. Miss Broder, her Aunt Bernette, caught up with her, putting an arm around her shoulder. Fedalia could hear her crying.

CHAPTER THIRTY

Adelbert closed both eyes as he put his thumb and forefinger in the corners, pinching hard on the bridge of his nose. He sighed heavily. "I shouldn't have listened to you last night, Helen. For once you were wrong. . . . I should have followed her right home and explained everything right then. Now I can't even find her."

He opened his eyes, and Helen's look made him feel like a demented child.

"Mr. Wixberry. What makes Fedalia the most unforgettable girl you ever met—you and everybody else who's ever seen her?"

Adelbert straightened up. He looked his secretary in the eye. "She's not a girl, she's a woman. No, she's not a woman, she's an angel—a child—a child-angel."

"You're warm, Mr. W. She's a full-blown girl-woman who has never lost the simple uncomplicated perspective—or focus, or whatever you want to call it—of a child—the thing you and I and everybody else had when we were four and then lost somewhere along the way in the puzzlement of growing up in a world where the inhabitants continually say things they don't mean, act nice to people they hate, and vice versa, lose face, lose poise, become embarrassed, lie in each other's teeth, open their mouths in——"

"What are you trying to prove?"

"I'm trying to point out to you that the only time in her life Fedalia didn't make crystal-clear common sense was when her father sent her off to New York on a wild-goose chase. She has now, thanks to your high principles and your high-frequency voice, got straightened out; and if you could just shake off the complicated mental gymnastics we so-called human beings employ to confuse every issue, you could figure out, without leaving this room, exactly what simple, clear, honest, and logical move Fedalia is making right this minute."

Analyzing Fedalia was beside the point as far as Adelbert was concerned. "I've got to find her, and find her quick, and explain all those things she heard me say."

"There you go. For once Fedalia heard somebody say something honest, and you want to go back over it and give her a messed-up version of the same thing that won't make any sense to her at all. Sure she's hurt, but now she understands, and she's got the courage to take it. The first thing she would do is get back to Fort Madison and start over, and I'll bet you forty thousand dollars she's on her way there this minute. She'll send us both post cards the first stop the train makes, and my advice to you, Adelbert, considering my advice is personal and not business, is to relax. Now, Mr. Wixberry, this is not Friday, but a young lady was promised an audition yesterday which she didn't get to give, due to circumstances entirely beyond her control. Remember?"

Adelbert was so dumfounded at hearing Helen call him by

his first name that the next thing he knew she was calling the audition room to proceed. "I'll just turn the speaker on and have it ready," she said with what struck him as a cozy sort of smile.

"Well, keep the volume low, will you?" he growled.

He started pacing, and some five or six minutes went by during which time he made himself actually listen to a very mediocre voice. Then he sat down. "Helen, call the audition control room and have them send that so-called artist in here."

He enjoyed Helen's eye-popping as she said incredulously, "Do what?"

"Call the audition control room and ask them to send that singer we just heard over here to my office." As Adelbert repeated the remark he was entirely aware of the patient quality in his voice so foreign to these walls. He waited calmly at his desk, and presently a frightened, colorless face preceded a shaking little body into the outer office. Adelbert thought, So that's what they look like every Friday. His throat tightened as he looked at the small figure trembling in the doorway.

"Come right in, Miss Grudd," Helen said. Miss Grudd just barely edged herself inside the door. "This is Mr. Wixberry."

"Well, Miss Grudd," Adelbert said, "I want to thank you for coming all the way down here to sing for us. Who is your teacher?"

Miss Grudd's mouth opened once and then shut and then opened again. She said, "Avnageecher."

"I beg your pardon, Miss Grudd?"

"Avnageecher," she said again.

"Oh, I see. You haven't got a teacher?"

Miss Grudd's head went up and down.

"Well, Miss Grudd. Let me say that many, many young ladies yearn to become big radio or opera stars, young ladies who believe sincerely that diligence and determination and

205

suffering are going to achieve that goal for them. But there is another element, Miss Grudd, a very important one, called talent. This is given to a very few, however, maybe only to one in a million—talent to become a fine singer, that is. Now if I were to tell you that I didn't think you had that necessary talent you'd probably feel like going out and shooting yourself, wouldn't you?" The head went up and down again. "Now, Miss Grudd, just suppose that out of every million aspiring souls, 999,999 young men and young ladies went out and shot themselves. Think of how bad off this world would be, losing all the talent those people unquestionably have for other things, like—well—like maybe winning blue ribbons with flowers, or possibly becoming artists in many other artistic fields. Mind you, Miss Grudd, I didn't say you didn't have singing talent, now did I?" Miss Grudd's head went from side to side. "I only say, in addition to enjoying the compliments of your folks and your friends, just keep your eyes and ears open while you're dreaming about how exciting it would be to sing on the radio or in the opera, and get yourself a nice broad view at other activities and other endeavors. It's good to be generally well informed in as many things as possible, and then if you decide that you fit even better into something else besides a singing career, you can make the switch without too much complication and—ah—disappointment. Come back and see me in six or eight months and we'll see what kind of improvement you've made and in which direction. Okeh, Miss Grudd? And good luck."

Miss Grudd swallowed and said, "Thangrichberry." Mr. Wixberry said, "You're welcome, Miss Grudd," as he smiled the young lady out of the office. She closed the door softly behind her. Adelbert walked around to the edge of his desk and sat down.

"Helen."

"Yes?"

"What was the idea of calling me by my first name a few minutes ago?"

"What else can I call you when we're talking about anything as personal as we were talking about?"

"You might call me by my nickname, in case we ever get into a real personal discussion."

"I don't want to call you anything that will remind me of that vile Pabalot female."

"My nickname happens to be 'Slugger.' You can ask your friend Spart Coliss next time he comes in. Which will probably be fairly soon, as he is one of my friends, too, one of my closest friends, in fact."

"You don't say!"

"I do say. And speaking of flowers, you know, Miss Jern, you're not built like a privet hedge at all. When I picked you up a while ago——" He cleared his throat. "So why do you dress like one?" He was pleased to see Helen turn pink as though she enjoyed blushing.

"Maybe I won't dress like one after this," she said.

CHAPTER THIRTY-ONE

"Teleegrams to all pernts," the nasal voices were saying, not now as strange-sounding to Fedalia as they had been in this same railroad station such a short time ago, when she had seen Uncle George for the first time.

She sat down with Aunt Bernette on one of the waiting-room benches where they could watch the clock.

"I hope you won't be too tired sitting up," Aunt Bernette said. "I could have spared the money for a berth if it had been later in the week."

"I'll be just fine, Aunt Bernette. And thank you so much for my sandwiches and the fried chicken and the cake and the can of milk for Raggy."

"I wish I could-a done more. Last night when you told me you were my sister's little Fedalia I just couldn't believe it. And now, sitting there, you look so much like my sister herself that I don't know why I didn't recognize you for her child the moment I clapped eyes on you."

"I can see how you look like Mama's pictures too. How old was she the last time you saw her, Aunt Bernette?"

"Just around your age, I guess. Eighteen, nineteen. My first husband only took me as a second choice when your mother married Luther Parker. But I was never in love with him like I was with George Broder. George had such a—oh, polished way. And he was a wonderful husband, too, except for spending every hour day and night with his science books. Hardly slept at all, but he was always kind and gentle till his sister died. Then he got all mixed up mentally and every other way. Three times he ran away from being committed, and every time I followed him, thinking I could keep him out of trouble. Several years back he started calling me Anne now and then. That's his sister's name. And about four months ago I guess he got to actually believing I was his sister. Well, if I was his sister, in his mixed-up head, then his wife must be dead. Anyway, he kept on calling me Anne. He hasn't called me Bernette since, till yesterday there in his office."

"What will they do to him, Aunt Bernette? If it doesn't upset you for me to ask——"

"No, Fedalia. He'd already been committed and was to go to the state hospital when he ran away to come here to New Jersey. So that's where he'll go. Back to the state hospital. I know I should have told where he was long ago. But I just kept hoping he'd get well, and I thought I could keep him out of trouble being nearby. I couldn't talk about it last night, but now I'm glad it's all over."

"What would he have done to me yesterday, Aunt Bernette? If you hadn't come to the office right then?"

"God knows, Fedalia. I only knew I had to turn him in and get over there as quick as I could. All I can tell you is that when Anne died—she was his twin, Fedalia. Did I tell you that? Well, Anne died from blood poisoning after a little scratch from a kitten. That was in New York State, just after we was married eight years ago. Anne suffered terribly, and George seemed to blame himself that all his books and scientific studies couldn't help her. When she died every good trait of George's seemed to—oh, get all out of kilter, in opposite directions, I guess you'd say. His gentle ways become carefully figured-out cruelty. And all that terrible pain he saw Anne suffer become twisted in his mind into something great and grand. Like some high power, I guess you'd say, that he had to respect and study, like a religion. But I loved him, Fedalia. I loved him so much that I couldn't let them take him. When I followed him here he told everyone I was his sister, so I never let on I was his wife. And I suspected everyone who come near. You were the first one who ever treated me like a human being in almost six years."

Fedalia patted her aunt's hand. "I think we'd better get over to the gate now."

Fedalia took hold of the telescope and the small brown bag. Aunt Bernette carried Raggy's box and the package of food. As they waited by the gate Aunt Bernette said, "I hope you'll write to me about the boys and how everything is at home."

"Of course I will, Aunt Bernette. And don't forget you promised to come out for a visit next summer. I don't see why you don't let the rooming house go and come to stay with us. I'm sure I can go back to the greenhouse. And the boys are both working. There'd be plenty, and it would be just wonderful having you live with us."

"Maybe I can, Fedalia. For a while I'd rather be back here where George is. Maybe later, we'll see."

The man at the gate was letting people through. He said Aunt Bernette could go to the platform. The train came in suddenly with a noisy rush, like the subway. In a few minutes Fedalia was on board, sitting next to the window.

As the train pulled out she waved through the glass until Aunt Bernette and the crowds of people and the Newark station and the site of the beginning and end of her Eastern career all passed from view.

CHAPTER THIRTY-TWO

The boys had been waiting at the depot and had proudly taken Fedalia home in Mr. Howell's taxi. How quickly young boys get big and awkward. They were both so relieved and excited about her being home, they let her kiss them again as they dashed off to their Saturday jobs.

Raggy had stayed quiet at first on the train, in a corner of the cardboard box, but squirmed and cried all the way from Chicago, reaching her small paws through the air holes in the cover, only stopping her frantic attempts to get out when she fell asleep from frightened exhaustion. The conductor grinned at Fedalia when he said, "What have you got in the box, your lunch?"

She said, "No, sir, a cat."

"Couldn't be a cat," he said, "because cats aren't allowed on this coach." He was looking right at one of Raggy's paws waving out of an air hole when he said it. "I guess it's your lunch all right," he said, still grinning as he went down the aisle.

But now, after cautiously sniffing every corner of the house and scrupulously washing away every trace of her saucer of milk and her long journey, Raggy was curled up happily asleep in a patch of sunlight on the parlor floor.

As tired as Fedalia was from the long hours in the coach, she couldn't wait another moment to get at the dirty kitchen floor. The unpacking could wait. She found one of her old cover-up aprons right where she'd left it, pinned up her hair with a wiping towel, and was just turning the water into warm suds when the doorbell rang. She got up off her knees and hurried to the door. *It couldn't possibly be Charlie. He'd be at the drugstore, and besides . . .*

"Good morning, madam," a thin cheerful little man in a derby hat said to her. "Are you the lady of the house?"

"Yes, sir," Fedalia said.

"Then - may - I - show - you - direct - from - the - home - office - for - demonstration - purposes - only - the - Golden - Era - combination - table - phonograph - and - radio - which - can - at - the - touch - of - your - hand - fill - the - home - with - drama - mirth - excitement-and-glorious-music——"

"Excuse me," Fedalia said. "I'm in the middle of scrubbing the kitchen floor. But I think I'd like a machine that could allow me to listen to glorious music while I'm doing other important things."

"Yes, madam-ah-then-may-I-show-you-direct-from-the-home-office - for - demonstration - purposes - only - the - Golden-Era-combination-table-phonograph——"

"Excuse me," Fedalia said. "If you could come back in about three months, I think I may have the money saved up for a small down payment. At the present time——"

The gentleman made a note in his order book. "That will

be quite satisfactory, madam. May I wish you good day?" He lifted his hat, smiled, and stepped off the porch and down the walk.

Fedalia went back to the kitchen and had just dipped the brush into the pail when she heard more footsteps on the porch. *It couldn't be Charlie. Not possibly, because in the first place* . . .

"Fedalia!" the postman said. "I wondered if you could be home when I see this letter addressed to you. How are you, anyway? It's from New York."

"Mr. Woods! It's sure like home to see you, Mr. Woods. I only came home this morning and thought I better tidy up right away. Thank you." She dried her hands on her apron and took the letter.

"Well, now, are you going to stay for a while? Too bad about Red passing on."

"Yes, I am, Mr. Woods. Thank you for your sympathy. I guess it was just meant to be."

"I know," Mr. Woods said on an inhale. He wiped out his gray cap with his handkerchief. "Pretty warm for October. Well, I'll see you, then. The boys well?"

"Just fine, Mr. Woods. Thank you." He shifted his big leather bag and started off the porch. Fedalia went back to the kitchen, opening the letter carefully. There was no beginning or end to the one typewritten page.

> Every day, sure as the sunrise,
> There's somebody falling in love—
> And every evening by the very same token
> Vows are whispered that are never broken.
> Every day, sure as the sunset,
> There's danger of you falling too—
> I'd love to hold you in my arms till you do—
> Every day.

Fedalia looked out through the back entry at the last of the fall colors in the yard. She could hear Jody Sutlough yelling at the postman from next door. "Look at me, Mr. Woods. Look at me. Up here in the tree!"

She got down on her knees again and dipped the brush in the warm water. The front doorbell gave a short ring that startled her because she hadn't heard any footsteps on the porch. She dried her hands again. *It couldn't be Charlie. He wouldn't even know she was back. And even if he did . . .*

She opened the door. Charlie's black curls were down over his forehead. His mouth was tightly shut, unsmiling. His eyes never left hers. She stepped back, bumping into the hall seat. He followed her, leaving the door open behind him. Slowly, it seemed, he put his arms around her. She felt his hand on the back of her head. He seemed taller than she'd remembered, her head tilting back against his hand. He didn't let her eyes go even when he pressed his lips on hers, full and warm and hard—and long. . . .

She spoke first after that, although the best she could do was whisper. "Charlie, why didn't you write? Even a postal card?"

Charlie could only whisper too. "I did write. To New Jersey."

"*Did* you, Charlie? I never got it."

"Why didn't you write me anyhow?"

"Because you didn't even come to the depot. Why didn't you, Charlie?"

He dropped his head, looking down in the small-boy way she remembered so well.

"I just couldn't, Fee. I sure tried, though."

"If you'd wanted to, you could have been there. You could do anything you wanted to, Charlie. Remember the cross-country? When Shink Burns fell down and you came on past him to win? Oh, Charlie, your face was so white and you were gasping so. I think I would have kissed you right there in front of everybody if I could have got through the crowd."

Charlie dropped down onto the hall seat, took her hand, and pulled her down beside him. "If you had," he said against her hair, "I would have fallen dead on the sidewalk." Suddenly he sat up straight, grabbing her shoulders, and turned her to face him. "Wait till I tell you about the drugstore! Mr. Gale said all along I had everything a good drugstore manager needed if I could only develop a little more cheerful personality. Well, wait till I get back to the store *now!* I'll have so much cheerful personality he'll have to tie me down, I guess!"

"Charlie, you mean you'll manage the store someday?"

Charlie nodded his head several times, fast. "That's the way Mr. Gale's been talking!"

Fedalia found herself wanting to kiss the eagerness around Charlie's eyes. "Oh, Charlie, I'm so glad you're going to be a druggist and not a track coach."

"Track coach! *Me?* Oh, Fee, I was never any good as a runner. I guess I was what you'd call a one-race Charlie. That's how I missed your train that Saturday night at the depot."

"How do you mean, Charlie?"

"Well, I thought I could make it to the depot on foot after the store closed, and I missed by three minutes. I couldn't even hear her whistle for the junction by the time I got there."

"Charlie! You tried to run all the way from Gale's Drugstore to the depot? Why didn't you take your bicycle?"

"There's no reason for me to tell you any of this, Fee——"

"Charlie Landry, *why* didn't you take your bicycle?"

"I just happened to sell it that afternoon to a kid who lives up on the North Side. He promised not to take it till the next day, but I guess he changed his mind because when I came charging out of the store after closing up my bike was gone."

"I should think Mr. Gale would have let you off a few minutes early."

Charlie cleared his throat, which didn't seem to need clearing. He moved around uncomfortably. "He wasn't there that night."

Fedalia jumped to her feet. "Charlie, you mean Mr. Gale wasn't there all evening?"

"Well, no, Fee, he wasn't feeling well and he left for home at noon. Why?"

"How much did you get for your bicycle, Charlie?"

"Well—now you see——" Charlie cleared his throat again. "I only got twenty dollars. She was worth a lot more with all the stuff I had on her, but I—well, I happened to want to make a quick sale, so I called this kid up and—oh—well. You see? That's how it was. So I ran to the depot——"

"Yes, Charlie, I see." Fedalia dropped down onto the seat. Charlie would be terrified at her crying, but she knew there was no use trying to hold the tears back. She clung to him tightly, trying not to sob or get his face wet. "Don't be scared, Charlie," she finally managed to say. "Girls like me generally cry a lot when they're glad."

She could feel Charlie frantically trying to get his handkerchief out of his pants pocket without loosening the fierce grip he had around her shoulders.

"Don't you blame Red now, Fee—I mean Mr. Parker. I asked him not to tell you it was me loaned the money. When he came to the store and found out Mr. Gale had gone home sick, he was so discouraged he told me all about not being able to get the last twenty dollars for your ticket. Of course the bank was closed by that time so I couldn't take anything out of my savings, so I just thought of the bicycle. That North Side kid's old man is a mechanic and he knew that bike was a steal for twenty bucks. So they brought the money right over and Red went on home, and that's how it was. I thought sure I could run to that depot in twenty-five minutes."

Charlie's handkerchief was wet through, but Fedalia's tears were dry. She knew Charlie would never have told her all the details if he hadn't felt it his responsibility to give her time to recover her poise. To show him she had recovered it she laughed and said, "Maybe Papa wouldn't have let me go to New York at all if you hadn't given him that twenty dollars. Maybe you're the one who actually sent me away, Charlie Landry."

Charlie looked so earnestly at her, she knew he'd taken her seriously. "I thought of that, Fee, but I knew my only chance was for you to get that singing out of your system. If you hadn't gone to New York you'd always have wondered."

She squeezed his hand. "Maybe I would have been a success, though, and never come home!"

He held onto her hand with both of his. "I had to take that chance, Fee, and anyway, I heard you sing quite a lot of times at church and different places—and I—well, honestly, Fee——"

"Honestly *what*, Charlie? Honestly you didn't think I could sing. Is that it, Charlie?"

He opened his mouth to answer and she waited. He swallowed and opened his mouth again, without saying a word.

"Honestly *what*, Charlie?" Fedalia said firmly.

Charlie finally found his voice. "Honestly, Fedalia," he said, "I—I love you."